Keegan

A savagely mutilated doll, the sinister reminder of the terrifying photos he had seen earlier in London, is in the shoe box given to Keegan as he embarks on the run from Belgium.

He has been 'sold' by his creditor, Viney, to a London firm to clear himself financially. But the firm has elaborate games in mind: games involving a patsy . . . International security is at risk. And the patsy, Keegan, is needed—dead.

Keegan:
The No-Option Contract

Brian Ball

WILDSIDE PRESS

For Harold and Madie

Published by
Wildside Press, LLC
P.O. Box 301
Holicong, PA 18928-0301 USA
www.wildsidepress.com

Wildside Press Edition: MMIII

The call was from Belgium, the caller urgent yet calm. Bromley listened carefully. At length, he said:

'What made you call us?'

'You pay quicker than the other agencies.'

'It's not our line.'

'It could be.' The caller explained, and Bromley began to smile. It was a neat scheme.

'I'll have to get it confirmed.'

'Mr Graves won't argue. He knows my information is always reliable.'

'Will you call back?'

'In one hour.' There was a pause, then the caller laughed. 'I take it he's in the sauna?'

'Thank you for calling,' said Bromley, replacing the receiver. He waited in the office for almost half an hour. Then the heavy green baize door on his right opened, and the Head of Section emerged. He looked as he always did at this time of the evening, both stimulated and enervated. 'A call from Eichstatt, sir.'

Graves huddled deeper into the swathes of purple towelling. Bromley considered his chief. It was an unpleasant sight. Graves had the look of an exotic and venomous reptile, leathery neck, scaled skin, obsidian eyes: blinking and toothless, yet possessed by a latent deadliness.

'I'm surprised he's still alive. The Israelis put a disposal order on him weeks ago. What's he got this time?'

'Five hundred rocket launchers for the Provisionals. By container lorry from Belgium. Routed to Liverpool, then Belfast.'

Graves poured himself a large gin and added lime-juice. 'Americans again?'

'Indirectly, sir.'

'Eichstatt wouldn't get in touch over a batch of rocket-launchers.'

'They are the latest thing, sir. Called the Skunk. A new

5

Canadian design.' Graves waited. 'No, it wasn't just an interception he had in mind, sir. Eichstatt had rather an intriguing idea.'

Graves listened. Eventually, he smiled.

'Anthony, it's made for us. We need something like this to show my Minister how efficient our operation is. The thing is, we'll need the shipment broken down into small parcels. If it goes through to Belfast, they might decide to keep it in a central cache, and that wouldn't do at all.'

Bromley waited. Graves finished his drink, wiped sweat from his wrinkled bald head.

'I think we'll put the word out that they've been rumbled. Use that journalist you know.'

'Rankin, sir.'

'Him. The drunk. I expect the Irish will be sending a minder?'

'Yes, sir. The driver's not in it. He's an employee of the container-rental firm. Hired with the container and transporter.'

'See he falls ill.'

'A switch, sir? I could find a professional. One of the internationals.'

'No. A professional would rumble *us*.'

Bromley saw the hard black eyes gleam with pleasure. Graves came fully alive when he was contemplating the death of another.

'A patsy?'

'Exactly, Anthony.'

'Find someone. Not stupid. Enough guts to make it look good. Now, leave me alone and get in touch with some of your villainous friends. You can pass the word that if they find the right man we'll arrange for the law to look the other way the next time they're caught scrumping apples.'

'I take it the driver's expendable, sir?'

'You take it aright, Anthony. Arrange it.'

THURSDAY

Keegan hauled on the brake and switched off the old lorry's creaking, rumbling engine. So the differential hadn't packed

6

up yet. With luck it would hold up tomorrow and then the Bedford would be ready.

He saw his reflection in the wide-angle mirror as he swung down from the cab. The limestone dust veined the ridges and planes of his sharp-featured face. He smiled. Ruthie said he looked like a stone-man. He wondered why she wasn't running across the waste ground to meet him. Any other day she'd have heard the grinding of the clapped-out Dodge and come yelling with her friends that her Dad was back.

Not today.

The local kids regarded unlocked cars and lorries as public property. In the morning he might find the cab littered with cans and used sheaths or stinking of urine.

Keegan didn't think of this, though. He thought of beer, hot water, a razor and the steak he had bought. Two minutes each side. Ruthie would watch whilst he shaved.

He strode across the cindered waste ground, a tired and fairly happy man. Seven round trips logged today. Another forty-five pounds in credit at Sheffield Lime Quarries. Money in the bank. Keegan's green eyes filled with pleasure.

The house was silent.

Keegan heard kids bawling to one another from the back of the terraced houses. A dog yelped as a child shot out of an entry on a new scooter. Keegan felt a moment of alarm.

He pushed the door open. It gave on to the small cluttered living-room.

'Ruthie!'

She was sitting in his chair, small, blonde as him, self-possessed, a hostess on her dignity.

'There's a man to see you,' she said. Very polite.

He had his back to Keegan. He turned. Young, thin, smartly dressed, blue suit, pale blue tie, pale blue handkerchief, tanned face, a big smile.

'Hello, Mr Keegan!'

He was up and offering to shake hands, the smile bigger and very sincere.

'My name's Perrin, Mr Keegan.'

'I made him a cup of tea, Dad.'

'You did right, love,' said Keegan. She'd brought out the uncracked cups.

7

'She's made me very welcome,' said the young man. 'You can be proud of Ruthie here!'

Ruthie. Keegan didn't like the use of the pet-name for his daughter.

'What was it?'

'Oh, just by way of business, Mr Keegan! Just a little chat – won't take a minute.'

Keegan saw how proud of herself Ruthie was. She'd have sent her friends away, even her best friend Helen, to do the entertaining bit. He didn't want to send her away.

'Get some potatoes from the corner shop,' he told her. 'And lard.'

'We've got potatoes.'

'Peas then. We're having steak.' He gave her a pound note. 'There's a good girl, Ruth.'

Perrin watched her go.

'Lovely girl,' he said. 'Does she favour her mother?'

Keegan's face hardened.

'What is it?'

He knew, though. Perrin was their messenger boy.

'It's your monthly accounts, Mr Keegan.' Perrin smiled, as if apologizing.

Keegan felt anger building up inside him. A messenger boy. But in a hundred-pound suit. Gold watch, silk tie, hair styled. He stank of money.

'So I couldn't pay it all.'

Perrin snapped open a thin brief-case and showed him an accounts sheet.

'February,' he said. 'Eighty pounds short.'

'There was no work! Every site in Yorkshire was on strike!'

'March. A hundred and three pounds short. We sent a reminder.'

'I sent what I could!'

Keegan caught the reek of perfume. They called it after-shave lotion: *perfume.*

'We sent more reminders.' Perrin counted. 'Six. And no money since the eighth of April.'

Keegan looked about the room. All of the furniture had passed through several hands. Torn fabrics, dusty curtains, a bare scuffed table. Ruthie was beginning to notice. She mentioned the new carpet at Helen's. Twice.

'I had trouble with the transmission. They couldn't get the parts for weeks.'

'We did specify prompt payment when the loan was negotiated.'

'You know I'll pay! I'm using the old Dodge – it shouldn't be on the road, but I'll pay.'

'Ah, but when, Mr Keegan?'

'As soon as I can!'

Perrin shook his head.

'You signed a contract, Mr Keegan. Our firm is quite insistent that we have no bad payers.'

Keegan felt the ache in his knee. It had been a long day at the wheel. Fifty, sixty miles an hour on the country lanes. Load up, blast on, deliver. All the time, the engine grunting like a sick pig.

'I've over a hundred pounds at the Quarry.'

'We'll have that.'

'All right.'

'And the rest.'

'I haven't got it!'

Perrin put the sheets away.

'Mr Viney was very insistent.'

Keegan wondered how Perrin would fall if he tapped him on his neat blue waistcoat. Perrin smiled, recognizing the impact of his message.

'Very insistent, he was. He said I should tell you he's taking a personal interest in your account.'

Keegan heard Ruthie's step at the door. He looked straight into Perrin's eyes.

'Tell him I'll pay him when I can.'

Perrin smiled. He was a charming smiler. Ruth came in.

'Dad, Helen's cat's just—'

She stopped. Keegan didn't learn what had happened to Helen's cat.

'Thanks for the tea, young lady!' Perrin called. 'You're a lucky man, Mr Keegan. I wish I had a girl like that.' He said, still smiling, 'Eight hundred and twenty-seven pounds. By Friday, Mr Keegan. Please.' Then he turned. 'By six.'

9

Ruthie watched him go.

'Didn't he smell lovely!'

'Didn't he.' said Keegan. Immediately he knew he had, puzzled Ruthie by his tone of voice.

'Well he did!'

Keegan forced a smile. 'Lovely, Ruthie. Now get that steak under the grill. We won't bother with potatoes.'

'What did Mr Perrin want, Dad?'

Keegan's face betrayed nothing.

'He was just asking about business, love. Nothing much. Just a bit of business about the lorry.'

'Has Dougie finished the repairs on the Bedford, Dad?'

It didn't matter whether Dougie had finished or not. The Bedford wasn't more than a quarter paid for, and Viney wanted his money. Suddenly Keegan wanted to get roaring drunk, just like the old days. Drunk, stupid drunk with maybe a couple of plates of curry and afterwards a hard-faced chippie from one of the clubs. Ruthie was watching him.

'If you don't get that steak on soon, I'll eat you.'

'*Dad!*'

Keegan was reluctant to leave Ruthie on her own. He called next door at the Singhs and asked one of the older girls if she'd look in a couple of times. The girl's great brown eyes followed him, he could feel their curious almond warmth on his back all the way across the cindered ground.

His first call was at a pub only a hundred yards away. It was quiet, between the six o'clock swill and the port-and-lemons of the old dears from the back-to-backs when the early T.V. weepies were over.

'Harry been in?' he asked the barman.

'In Majorca. Didn't you know?'

'No.'

'What'll it be?'

Keegan was already on his way out. You couldn't win them all, but Harry Carrick had been a good chance. He was one of the old gang from the days when the clubs took money so fast they didn't know what to do with it. Harry had set up as a bookie and sold out when the combines started. He owed Keegan favours. But he was living it up in the Mediterranean.

He made for a bus and in half an hour was ringing the doorbell of a small modern house near Handsworth.

'Hello, Mrs Cavendish,' he said to the bent old woman at the door. 'Where's Eric tonight?'

'Here!'

Eric Cavendish hulked in a doorway. He was big, a big frame loaded with fat.

'How's the lad! Haven't seen you for two months. Come in - get Terry a beer, Ma!'

Ma Cavendish nodded and shuffled to the kitchen.

'To you, Terry,' Eric said when the beer was poured.

'Cheers, Eric.'

'Well, how's the lad?'

He hadn't much in the way of conversation. He learned a phrase and thought it did for socializing. He had been that way at school. He was big and muscular, wanting to be a fighter in the days when there were provincial fight-halls. No one told him he was slow and stupid.

'Busy,' said Keegan, drinking and wondering if he was wasting his time. Probably. 'I was looking for Harry Carrick.'

'*He's* all right! Away, isn't he?'

'Till Sunday.'

'I'm glad you've come! We'll have a night! Go to the dog-track, eh, Terry?'

'I was looking for Harry to see how he was fixed.'

Eric's amiable faced creased with worry.

'Fixed, Terry?'

Keegan tried to make light of it. He rubbed his thumb and finger. 'Fixed for cash.'

'He's all right!'

'I'm not.'

Eric began to understand.

'Well, Terry! Well, then! You had trouble with the lorry, didn't you? Don't worry about tonight - I've got plenty!'

Keegan sat back. It might be working out. He hadn't wanted to think of the alternative. Now, he might not have to.

Keegan put down the glass.

'How much?'

Eric reached for a wallet. It bulged with notes.

'See that! Old Eric's all right!'

Keegan held back the tremor that started at the back of his neck. Eric had a hundred, maybe a little over, in his wallet. He had always been a saver, hence the neat house, the tidy garden and the modern furniture. He cycled to his work at the pit and rarely went boozing. He hadn't married and for all his talk of gambling his maximum stake would be a pound. The fight-game had looked him over, tried him out and laughed.

'Eric, I need getting on for a thousand.'

'For the bloody dogs!'

'For Viney.'

Eric understood at last.

'Viney! Sharkey Viney?'

'The lorry.'

'You took money from Viney. Why, he'd not lend *you* money!'

'He did.'

Eric drank his beer.

'When?'

'Friday.'

'Tomorrow.'

Big Eric, with a punch like a trip-hammer and the speed of a dray horse, pushed his wallet across to Keegan. He didn't say anything. He got to his feet and went to a dresser. He came back with a savings book and an envelope.

'Sixty in that,' he said, pushing across the envelope. 'Hundred and seven in the wallet. Leave my Ma a few quid for housekeeping. I'll get the savings out tomorrow.'

Keegan sweated as he looked at the figure in the savings book. His vision blurred. Then he saw the balance: a hundred and fifty-six pounds something.

'Sorry, Terry,' said Eric. 'Just paid off the mortgage.' His big face showed alarm. 'Haven't you got any?'

'About a hundred due.'

'Can't you sell anything?'

Keegan got to his feet.

'Eric, can you drop the rest in tomorrow? Through the letterbox. Soon as you can.'

'Will Ruthie be in?'

'She'll be at school.'

'Friday, he said?'

'Friday. By six.'

'Maybe I can raise some money on the house—'

It would take days.

'You've done enough,' said Keegan.

'What about the rest?'

Keegan looked at the money in his hands.

'I'll get it.'

'I'd like to smash his face in!'

Keegan nodded. They both knew Eric wasn't up to it. Anyway, Viney didn't do his own dirty work.

The next call was another pub. Keegan was greeted respectfully. He asked for Scarface and was sent to the posh bar. Scarface was a car-thief. He stole only medium-sized saloons eight years old and upwards. Scrap merchants took them without looking too hard. They were in bits within hours. It wasn't a big trade, but it was steady.

'Viney?' he asked, his old eyes rheumy, full of the day's booze. 'You didn't get mixed up with Viney? How much anyway?'

'About five hundred.'

'Not a chance.' Quite definite. 'Twenty maybe, thirty if you like.'

Keegan took it.

'Times are hard,' he said. 'And watch it, Terry. He still doesn't like you. Apart from the money.'

There was no one Keegan could borrow from in the next pub or the next. He tried three clubs, but one wouldn't let him in and the others were almost empty.

By closing time he realized that he had tried everyone who might possibly lend him money. Except for Harry Carrick, who would be home a week after Viney had sent his mob in to collect.

He walked home from the city centre, looking in shop windows and wondering about the sheer wealth of a large modern city. Every car that passed him represented more than he needed. In one shop window, electrical goods to a total of four thousand pounds sparked back at him.

13

There was a watcher in the shadows, moving.

Keegan caught the movement and turned on his bad knee. He ignored the sudden jolt and met the unknown.

'For fuck's sake, Terry!' bawled Scarface.

Keegan held back the punch.

'Come in.'

There was no sound from upstairs. Ruthie was a confident, nerveless sleeper. The bad times were in her baby days and she had few memories of them.

'Terry, it's the bit of loot you wanted.'

Keegan sweated, tongue-tied with hope. Scarface was another who owed him a favour. He had been caught cheating the table in the club where Keegan was the bouncer. He had to make it look good, for that was his job, but it was all superficial. Knuckle cuts, a jab with the elbow, lots of blood but nothing permanent. And Scarface knew it.

'What did you bring?'

'Oh, not money – hey, wait, lad! It's a dead cert!' He was very excited, full of booze. Keegan hoped the Ford outside wasn't stolen.

'What's a dead cert?'

'This garage! Easy! I know they keep all the petrol money overnight – and there's the wages!'

'You're moving up.'

'Not me! But a big fellow like you – if we got stopped, you could belt them one and we'd be away! The safe would go in the boot and—'

Suddenly Keegan could stand the little man's enthusiasm no longer.

'Go home.'

He was resentful, golden dreams fading.

'You've done time.'

'Not for thieving.'

He still tried to hold to his dreams. Keegan saw it.

'I'm not bent, and I'm not thieving!' he told Scarface.

'It's a bloody cert!'

He saw Keegan's face and stopped.

'Viney's a sod,' he said quietly.

'Yes. Go home.'

'Run for it.'

14

Keegan almost lost control.

'*Where!*' but he said it quietly.

Keegan pretended it was a normal morning. Ruthie's friends came at eight as they always did, full of talk, interesting zany kids' talk. When they left he packed a battered old case for her. He dressed carefully in the suit which wasn't too badly worn. Narrow trousers, narrow lapels. A sixties suit. The shoulders were tight, the belly-band slack.

He looked at the string-bound case and thought of toys. Then he found a plastic shopping-bag and stuffed it with dolls and crayons and comics. After that, he took a bus to the National Westminster Bank.

He had never been in a bank manager's office before.

Money wasn't unfamiliar, not if you'd been in on the huge flood of gambling fever that came when they took the lid off games. It hadn't seemed like money though.

The bank manager was a large, bespectacled young man, younger than Keegan.

'Now, Mr Keegan, you say you're in business?'

Keegan explained. He answered questions. No, he couldn't show any proper accounts. He had some papers from the tax people but not with him. No, he didn't own his house. No car? Keegan thought about the Dodge and almost smiled. He explained about the Bedford. It would be on the road soon.

The purpose of the loan?

Keegan remembered a phrase from the club days.

'I want to extend the business.'

He meant I want to keep Viney's goons in their cages. A handshake and he was outside, the pleasant reassuring words in his ears. They'd be glad to handle his account and later, who knows?

It was eleven o'clock.

Seven hours.

He tried the merchant bank. They were less polite.

He could have given up and got drunk, but there was still hope. The telephone, for instance. Old friends he had remembered in the long hours of early morning whilst he watched the sunlight filtering through the ragged curtains.

*   *   *

15

Unofficially, the Section didn't exist. Its funds came from a deep underground stream that eventually led to the river of public taxation, but so deviously only one man had worked out quite how, and he was dead. It was its own reason for its existence, made its own rules, worked directly for one Minister who was rarely a man to have more than a general idea of its actions; and certainly not of its methods.

Graves had set it up. Former (and now deceased) members of the Section swore he'd spied in the golden days of British Intelligence when the Kaiser was the enemy. He worked mostly through mercenaries, keeping two permanent members on his staff, an aide and a killer, both recruited for their unswerving obedience. He disliked initiative. It made the Section vulnerable.

'There are five possibilities,' said Bromley. 'All with form, all with obligations to do as they're told. All with the necessary licences, three speak enough German or French—'

'One of them.'

'Again, one of those has recently been arrested in France—'

'Not him.'

'So it leaves us with two, both suitable, both tough or at least competent.'

'Availability?'

Bromley checked.

'One due back from a trip Saturday midday.'

'The other?'

Bromley shrugged. 'He's not likely to be in fit shape for a few days.'

Graves rested his hands on his slight paunch. 'Which one might take the fancy of the Honourable Cynthia Haydon?'

Bromley laughed.

'They're not using that crazy cow as expediter are they?'

Graves wasn't amused.

'Don't be irreverent about the nobility. Which one?'

Bromley looked again at his list.

'I'd choose this one, but he's in his forties. Too old for Cynthia.' He reflected. 'When do you want the patsy ready?'

Graves yawned.

'Saturday evening. In Belgium.'

Bromley re-read the information on his list.

'This one's about right but he's due a going-over tonight.'

'Stop it.'

'I can't! It looks bad!'

'Then make sure he can drive afterwards.'

Bromley sighed his displeasure but Graves knew that Bromley would fix it. That was his job.

'He's to think we're mobsters. Hoodlums, Anthony.' Graves chuckled, an evil sound. 'After all, isn't that what we are?'

Keegan tried the manager's office at the third division club he had once played for. A youth hadn't even heard of a Mr McBride. Nor the old coach, Wally Lansden. No addresses, nothing, even when Keegan got through to a woman clerk he had known.

Keegan took a taxi back to the terraced house in Attercliffe. Suddenly it was important to make sure that Eric had left the hundred-odd pounds. It was there, with a badly-spelt note. 'I'm working. Let me now if theres anything ells. Sod Viney.'

There was the money at the quarry company to fetch. Keegan drove up in the grunting Dodge and had to wait around for the tally clerk to come back from his lunch. He argued about paying in cash, but he knew the contract drivers. They would make life difficult for him if he made them wait.

Keegan counted. With what Eric had left it came to four hundred and sixty-six pounds.

Over four hundred short. Three o'clock.

Keegan drove carefully to the school. He hadn't long to wait.

Ruthie came out at one minute past four, long legs flashing and small face split into a grin that reminded him agonizingly of her mother. He waved from the cab.

'Dad! Can I have a ride in the Dodge? Can Helen come and Jean and—'

'No, we're away to your Auntie's.'

'Oh, no!'

Auntie Edie, Keegan's mother's sister, lived eight storeys

up a block of gleaming new flats. She was a cantankerous drunken old cow, and Ruthie rightly loathed her; but she was the only relative Keegan could claim.

Keegan didn't disclose that Ruthie was staying overnight and maybe a good deal longer, depending on the goons' orders, but Ruthie knew when he brought out the string-bound suitcase and the plastic bag. She argued until he said she had to stay, and then she wouldn't talk to him, tight-lipped and distressed.

Aunt Edie was worse, but not drunk. When they watched him hurry away they both looked worried.

Keegan drove a few streets away and tried to ring Viney.

He raised one office but they wouldn't talk. Girls with calm, clear voices routed him to untroubled, alert and confident men. Perrin was at the third number but it had taken nearly an hour.

Almost five o'clock.

'Get me Viney.'

'Ah, is it Mr Keegan? He *will* be pleased that you've called! We'll be along for the money. Not me, ha ha.'

Smiler. Laughing. Excited now.

Keegan looked at his fist, the one that held the telephone. He would put up a show. Not too much, so they wouldn't bust his kidneys. They'd have to put him in hospital, or Viney wouldn't be able to sustain his reputation. It was a delicate business, just how much resistance to put up.

'I've got four hundred and sixty-odd,' he said.

'Oh, Mr Keegan, that isn't the right sum at all! How *have* you been doing your sums?'

'Get me Viney.'

'Now you know Mr Viney's a busy man!'

'I'll call him at home.'

Perrin wasn't worried.

'Try it, Mr Keegan,' he said. 'You won't get through. He's ex-directory, of course. Anyway, what do you think Mr Viney wants to talk to you about. It's just business, Mr Keegan!'

Keegan slammed the phone down.

It was more than business. For years Viney had wanted a chance to set his goons on him. Everyone would say Viney was right. Keegan owed money. Viney was entitled to collect. Keegan breathed in slowly.

He could take precautions of course. A crutch-box. Shin-pads. A couple of thick sweaters doubled back over his liver and kidneys and spleen. Just like Third Division again. The Dodge ran as sweet as honey all the way back to the cindered waste ground.

Keegan waited in the house with the door open.

Six o'clock passed. Minutes crawled. What were they trying? Curry smells drifted in from next door. Some people didn't like Indians for neighbours.

Seven came, then eight. Keegan sat and waited. It was ten before he gave up. He hadn't eaten since morning and then only to show Ruthie that this was another normal day. He went out for fish and chips and a bottle of beer. That's all, he told himself: I'm going out for food and beer.

The chip shop blazed on a corner two hundred yards away. Keegan knew approximately where they would be waiting. He walked quickly, head down, pads pressing against his shins.

'Hello-ee,' said a voice from the alley.

Keegan turned, and another voice called:

'Keegan!'

He saw the first caller, a gaudy youth, purple suit, yellow tie, and, of all things, a straw hat. Keegan laughed aloud. The youth had a brick in his hand. Beside him, a squat, older man.

Keegan caught another movement. Three men. He wished he had thought of heavy boots. Quarrymen's boots with steel toe-caps.

He thought, mouth dry, I'll hit that one, the youth, make sure he doesn't brain me with that brick. I shouldn't have laughed, he's the danger.

'Money, Keegan,' said the squat man.

Keegan didn't know him. Short, ugly, older than most heavies, Geordie by the sound of him, broken nose, a fighter?

'I've got four hundred-odd,' he said.

The man behind the Geordie emerged from the shadows. Keegan knew him from the club days. He couldn't remember his name. He'd worked in Leeds for Viney. And he'd been at the club where Tina used to peddle cigarettes and con the fat businessmen.

'Give,' said the old hand.

'And?'

'I break your legs,' said the youth with the brick. He was nearer.

Keegan felt a stab of remembered pain through his right knee. The ligaments. They never got better.

'I told Viney I raised some money!' said Keegan, not needing to pretend panic. The youth meant it. He was tall and slim but well-muscled, one of those deceptive frames, all bone and sinew, like an old-fashioned right-wing, built for bustle and speed.

'Keegan, Mr Viney said you hadn't paid,' said the man whose face was familiar. 'He didn't say you could just walk away owing him money, did he, Geordie?' No, said the Geordie. 'Did he, young un?' No, said the youth, he did fuck.

Things had changed.

'You don't hit me with that,' Keegan said to the youth.

'Oh, I do, Keegan,'

He swung very quickly and Keegan almost missed the flight of the raw-edged half-brick. Instinctively he leapt high as the youth moved, high right, left leg arching full of power though only with the weight of lightweight summer shoes to drive into the youth's crutch. It was enough. Brick-boy slammed into the wall and Keegan hadn't got his balance before the others swarmed forward, belting away without much science because they were as afraid as him, no coolness, no pre-determined attack, wild swings from shoe and fist and so many of them that Keegan had to collect *some*.

Keegan cannoned off a wall with coldness flooding his left thigh. He fell into a fore-arm smash to the side of his head, but he didn't go down. He couldn't. The squat goon was holding him up, trying to put a knee in his groin.

The youth gurgled unhappily. His mates got busier, both of them grunting. Keegan saw sheet lightning, through it the youth crawling. He had found his half-brick. It was funny in a way, his obsession with it. Keegan's mind was swimming. He wasn't hitting out much.

20

A well-directed blow from Geordie caught him full in the mouth. Teeth grated, none snapped. Lucky. Panicking, Keegan tried to raise his left leg to scrape it down the squat man's leg, a nasty trick to take the skin off. He hadn't got the strength.

Brick-boy was almost on his feet.

The bastard's going to do it, thought Keegan. He's too young to stop himself. *He wants to break my legs!*

A last effort brought nothing.

Viney had waited five, six years for this, the undisputed right to break him. Legitimately. Break bones with no come-back for when you'd been hard, lived Viney's way, you couldn't go running to the boys in blue.

It was Viney, however, who stopped it.

Keegan hadn't heard him arrive. He might have been watching from the start for all he knew.

'Let him go,' Viney said quietly. There was reluctance in his voice. Keegan started to fall as arms and torsos moved away. 'Hold him up.'

Through the blood-haze and pain Keegan saw Viney. The years had deposited a lot of flesh and a serene expression. Nothing worried Viney. He had all the things he'd schemed, grafted, killed for. Money. Position. Power. Everything except Tina, Keegan's one-time wife.

Keegan tried to stop the trembling. The third heavy was shaking too. Keegan had him placed now. Gus. Gus something. Gus had known Tina.

'Let me tear his balls off,' croaked the young man. He'd seen too many gangster films. The half-brick was his style.

Viney looked at him.

'Why don't you go and play with your dollies?'

The youth glared for a moment and then was sick.

'Well, Vic?' said Keegan.

Viney shone a torch into Keegan's face.

'You didn't pay.'

Keegan tried to put his hand into his pocket. The arm was afire. He fought down the instinct to keep it from further hurt and dragged out the envelope.

'Four hundred and sixty-six.'

21

'Not enough.' He took the envelope.

Keegan struggled with words. He wanted to say that he would work off the rest if he was given a chance, but Viney wasn't going to give him any time, none at all. It was in his eyes.

Without meaning it as an apology, Keegan said:

'She doesn't matter now, Vic. She's—'

Viney's thin lips almost vanished in his tight rat-trap of a mouth. His shadowy face thrust forward.

'Don't mention her! Don't even *think* of her!'

Keegan couldn't feel any sense of triumph. He had taken the only woman Viney felt anything for, and she had turned out to be a poisonous bitch full of heat and venom, crazy after a few months to have them fight over her.

'I haven't seen her for years, Vic—'

'Shut up!'

The goons tensed, not wanting to go in again. Keegan waited.

Gus looked at his battered hands.

'We shouldn't hang around too long, Vic.'

Viney controlled himself.

'I've good news for you Keegan. You're off the hook.'

Keegan couldn't order his thoughts. There was murder in Viney's shadowy face, but his words said something else. Warning bells clanged in his head. Viney had blamed him for Tina's sudden and abrupt reversal to the vicious and predatory animal she had been before her swish club days. Long after she had left him, Keegan learned that Tina had been on the game at thirteen. In a small way. In a shed. Mostly with Pakkies.

After four months of marriage with him, Tina had found her way into a call-girl syndicate. That was the clincher when it came to the custody of Ruthie. Quietly, the Welfare people had supported Keegan's claim, quietly they had told Tina not to press hers.

'Vic, we shouldn't hang around,' said Gus.

'Get him in the car.'

They hustled Keegan. He half-resisted, but his strength hadn't returned. There was the right leg. A mouth full of blood. A dull throb from the crack against the wall. Other things, chest wall and belly. Not bad. At least Ruthie hadn't seen the working over.

Keegan tried to forget his injuries. When they were near the motorway roundabout he swallowed a clot of blood and said:

'Where to, Vic?'

Viney didn't answer.

Keegan felt strength returning. He felt panic too, but he thrust it down. Viney was a killer. How he had disposed of a couple of envoys from some London mob was widely known. They lay entombed under a Leeds office block. There were other rumours too, one about a woman: a packing-case weighted with lead, and a sea-trip.

Keegan shifted position.

Viney said calmly:

'Don't look so worried, Keegan. I said you're off the hook.'

Keegan tried to move his arms. Viney sighed.

'I'll tell you,' he said. 'All I know. That's fair enough, isn't it?'

They were doing a steady sixty. Easy and steady, no haste, the big Ford was very smooth. Keegan thought of Ruthie and struggled once. Gus put an elbow to his neck. He showed Keegan the glinting blade.

'Don't, Terry.'

'You're going to see a man who wants a job doing,' said Viney. 'Two of his men will take you to London. Do the job properly and you're in the clear. You'll owe me nothing.'

Keegan nodded. Time enough to argue when he was away from the knife.

He made it sound good:

'All right, Vic. What job?'

'Driving.'

'Cars? What, a hijack?' He had been offered jobs in the club days. Once, because he had impressed by his skill, a small driving job in a bank raid.

'Nothing like that.'

'And the money I owe, it's off the slate?'

'The whole lot.'

Keegan felt pleased suddenly, and then realized how

stupid it was. For a moment, he had visualized himself clear of the crippling interest repayments on the Bedford, with enough work to get out of the rat-infested slum.

'So I get the Bedford if I do the job? I still owe you three years' payments.'

Viney knew he had never been bent. It was a con. But Keegan wanted to get out of the car, away from the knife, feet on the ground, bright lights and people around him.

'You've had your ration for not paying,' agreed Viney. Very calm, almost purring.

'And this man who wants—'

'He's a big wheel. London.'

Keegan couldn't keep the worry from his voice.

'How long will it take?'

'Forty-eight hours.'

The weekend. Ruthie would be fine. Maybe she'd have to stay at Auntie Edie's till Monday, even Tuesday. But she wouldn't be away from school long enough for the Welfare people to start worrying. The big car was very comfortable. Keegan tried to relax.

Keegan almost missed it when the Geordie slid the car in at the back of the dark lorry park. He was used to parking amongst the rigs. His injuries startled him into realization though.

'What are we doing—'

'Shut up,' said Viney. 'Don't get chicken. Nothing's going to happen.'

The Geordie kept the engine running.

After two minutes, a dark shape rolled up. *Mercedes*, registered Keegan. He tried for the number-plate but there wasn't enough light. None on the car, none in the lorry-park. He made out two figures. So Viney hadn't lied about that part of it.

The trouble was, whose men were those in the Merc? Keegan was recovering fast. The pain had turned into the nagging ache that meant returning strength, the muscles and bones complaining but acknowledging that they would try. In Third Division soccer, you were bounced, then you got up. No stretchers. You got up and played on.

Gus showed Keegan the knife again.

'He'll cut you if you try,' said Viney. He wasn't fooled by Keegan's show of co-operation. They had known one another well in the old days. If anyone had been a friend of Vic's, it was Keegan. That was why taking Tina had so hit him. That was why they were in the car now.

Keegan tensed. He watched two men get out of the Merc. One heavy and medium height, the other tall and thin. They waited.

Viney wound the window down.

Keegan heard a well-educated, calm voice coming from one of the men, he wasn't sure which:

'Just stay in the car, Mr Viney. Tell your man to come out.'

Gus started to get out.

'Still!' snapped the well-educated voice, and Keegan heard the authentic note of command.

'He's in the middle,' said Viney, a bit rattled. 'He can't get over Gus. He's damaged.'

'Then tell your man to get out slowly and put his hands on the car roof. He doesn't take a step nearer and he doesn't look this way.'

'Out, Gus. You heard,' said Viney. And in a low voice: 'Do it their way, Gus!'

'Now Keegan,' said the commanding voice.

Keegan stumbled out.

'Quite still!' whiplashed the voice, and Keegan knew it came from the tall thin one. Not old. Twenty-four, five. Gentleman mobster. Much more dangerous than Viney. A thin, intelligent face, dark hair, very alert. Suddenly Keegan had a memory of Viney scared before, when a nig found himself five pounds short on change from a tenner and the blackjack girl sneering at him. He was a big one and he'd made for Viney. Keegan had tripped him and hit him, not hard, on the neck, and that was the nig out cold. Viney was sweating. Not much, and no one else saw it. But Keegan knew.

Viney's face gleamed. A touch of fear.

'Drive away slowly, headlights dipped, then north and don't hang about,' said the well-educated voice.

The Ford swished away.

25

Keegan waited. There was nothing else to do.

'Listen, Keegan,' said the tall thin man. 'You're coming with us. You've got a job to do, and we know you've had a roughing up. Try to follow this. I could tap you on the head and you wouldn't wake up for three, four hours. Then you'd be slow and stupid, and we don't want that. Follow?'

'Yes.'

'You'll sit in the back with Nider here. Two and a quarter hours, maybe a bit longer. There's glucose and milk, hot, in a flask. Also a mild sedative. A pain-killer. It'll help you sleep but it won't leave any after-effects tomorrow.'

'Yes.'

Keegan glanced at the heavy-set man's face. Asiatic features.

'*Don't try it!*'

There was enough light for them to see the way he had set himself for a sprint. It was fifty yards to the lights of the diner, and he still had his speed when the ligaments held. He would have tried it, for he knew he had nothing to lose by doing so. The heavy-set man had moved to cut him off, very fast for a man of his bulk. An athlete, thought Keegan.

'Keegan, we're not going to harm you!'

'No.'

'I could have dropped you any time! I could have put a knife in you five minutes ago. Couldn't I?'

He sounded very reasonable.

'Yes.'

'I could have got Viney to put a wire around your neck and you'd be on a slab tomorrow. Right?'

Keegan felt laughter rising. He had a friend.

'Yes.' He kept the despair out of his tone.

'Keegan, I want you to trust us.'

'All right.'

'Nider's got a gun. Show him.'

Nider moved forward. He kept three fast strides away. Keegan had seen shooters before. This gleamed dull-black, the barrel long and too fat. *Silencer*, he registered. An automatic. You couldn't silence revolvers someone had said years back. Why not?

'I'm driving. Nider's going to sit next to you. We've got

26

rather a special kind of harness to make sure you don't try anything foolish. It won't be uncomfortable. Follow?'

Keegan got the picture. Himself trussed and doped. No need, really, for the silenced automatic. They were efficient and they didn't worry too much about consequences.

'Be sensible,' said Nider.

Nider sounded educated too, but not like the other.

'Yes,' said Keegan.

The thin man pretended to relax.

'Then we'll all be pals.' He kept the three strides that would make sure Keegan had no chance of getting to him before he could react. 'In and have a long drink. Nider will help with your reins. He'll shoot if you make a lot of fuss.' He said it very quietly, without emphasis. 'It would spoil my night to have to get rid of you.'

Nider held out the plastic cup. 'All of it,' he said. Keegan began to feel fear then. They weren't just efficient. They didn't *care*.

The car slid away as Keegan felt his senses going. The drug was quick-acting. He tried to keep awake, and then there was no point, no point in it at all. He dreamt vividly, crashing dreams until he was swayed painfully into semi-consciousness. He was vaguely aware of lights, the approaches of a city. Lights: noise: jerks, swaying, fast turns, low voices, glimpses of trees, an impression of walking and then a long peace.

SATURDAY

Graves yawned. His dentures clacked. 'How does he look to you, Anthony?'

Bromley shrugged.

'An oaf, but not stupid. He's wary and he's thinking.'

'You say he's a failure?'

'I should say that a good deal of the misfortune he's met with was contrived.'

Graves nodded. 'It sounds quite good.' He turned to the half-caste.

'What's your opinion, Nider?'

'He was off-balance last night, Mr Graves. He'd been done

27

over. He knew enough not to try anything in the state he was in then.'

'Bring him up,' said Graves. Nider and Bromley began to move. 'And show him some pictures.'

Nider's flat face became moon-like. He was smiling.

'The pictures we did in April, sir?'

'Yes. Give him a few minutes with them. He'll know we're not pussy-footing once he's had a good look at the late Mr Gilchrist.'

Keegan awoke to the gritty feel of rough blankets at his chin, so he kept his eyes tight closed and wondered how long it would be before he could have a drink or a woman or hear his daughter in the mornings; and then realized that he had served his time. But he was still in a cell.

It was past dawn, but not by much. He had slept. Five, six hours he guessed. They'd made no secret of the fact that he was a prisoner.

'In,' the tall thin one had said. Bromley, he'd called himself. *Mr Bromley.* Nider had remained Nider. Bromley asked if he needed plasters. Keegan checked. He had been roughed over but not hurt. Gus and the Geordie had blocked each other. Most Saturday games had left him as bruised. He'd stumbled through various doorways and then upstairs. A push, a door slammed. 'Don't wreck the furniture. There's no way out. We'll hear if you try, then we'll have to come and belt you. Get some sleep. You'll have to be up and about early.'

It was a smallish room, bleak and bare, with a metal-framed bed, a thin mattress and two blankets, a table and chair. Partitioned off, a lavatory and wash-basin. On the table, a meal of cold meat, bread, and a can of beer.

Keegan hated gaol.

He had gained full remission, but it still amounted to nearly a year of his life. The only visitors had been the Welfare people with news of Ruth.

There wasn't much to think of, so Keegan did what he had done in gaol. He made his mind a blank and thought of afterwards.

Afterwards, he would get away. When the hard bastards

28

who had frightened or bribed Viney made a slip. Carefully, for if they were big enough to put the push on Viney, they must be poison. Syndicate, if there still was a Syndicate operation in Britain.

Keegan put his shoes on and waited.

The birds were belting out their morning calls, and gradually the noise of traffic began to build up, not near though: subdued, at a distance. He was in London. North? The last few minutes of the journey were a hazy series of recollections. Definitely London. Keegan allowed himself to wonder what he was wanted for.

He had no illusions.

His only skills were driving and kicking a football, and when he had his leg nearly twisted off in an over-the-ball tackle against a visiting Italian team, he was finished. So he had taken the tests and settled to distance driving. The big rigs. At first in Britain, then over half Europe. Until Viney's offer. It had been too good to refuse. He wasn't called a bouncer. 'You'll be on our security staff,' Viney said. It had seemed a more exciting life than piloting machine tools to Hamburg, butter to Cardiff, frozen beef to Bruges. So why was he in London?

Keegan didn't think he had been driven to London to bounce drunks. It had to be driving. Bent driving. He would listen to the proposition and agree, no matter what. And then play it as it came. And out, as quickly as possible.

Footsteps, two sets, thudded on thin carpeting.

Keys rattled, and the door was flung back.

Bromley was there, with Nider.

Keegan examined both. Now that he could see Nider, he knew he had been right not to try to tackle the man. He looked much more competent than Viney's goons. There was a brooding violence about him that made Keegan watch him all the time. He was a half-caste, half Asian, but not thin-boned or delicate. He was of medium height and massively proportioned, with a wide neck edging into shoulders like sacks of flour. He carried a tray.

'Be sensible, Keegan,' said Bromley. 'There's toast and tea. When you've finished, you're coming to meet the boss. We don't want trouble.'

29

Keegan nodded. They were very careful. It wasn't the time, not yet. The tea was strong and sweet.

They took him downstairs, through an imposing room full of delicately wrought furniture, white and gilt. Keegan trod soft carpets, blue and gold. He felt no envy, for this was rotten money.

'Stop here,' said Bromley.

Keegan tensed. Nider was behind him, had been all the time. Something slapped in his hands. Keegan looked and saw the leather-cased cosh. A warning. Bromley slid back a wall-mounted display board.

Keegan didn't look at the photographs until Bromley said:

'He wanted to find out too much about us. Our chief wasn't pleased.'

Keegan looked. For a moment he thought it was dirty pictures, porno stuff, for the man was naked and tied to a chair. But the terror wasn't play-acting, and the blood wasn't ketchup. It wasn't kinky sex at all. The man had been slashed across belly and thin chest.

'Take a good look, Keegan.'

Keegan didn't want to look at the next picture, or the next. They were in sequence. Gradually the man became a *thing*. A wave of nausea and rioting fury swept through Keegan's big frame but before he could react and kick out backwards at the flat-faced bastard behind him, there was a hiss of air and Nider jabbed once, twice, at his kidneys. Not hard, but it stopped Keegan cold.

Through a roaring of hate and dread, Keegan heard Bromley's crisp upper-class voice telling him to calm down, calm down, be sensible.

In the last picture the man had no hands or feet. He was propped on the stumps, alive but not remotely human.

'Nider's quite an expert in his way,' Bromley was saying. 'This gentleman lasted eleven days. He didn't enjoy his stay with us, not at all. Keegan, are you paying attention? Mr Graves particularly wanted you to know what happens to unreliable chappies who don't follow orders.'

'This way,' said Nider. His voice was high, like a boy's. It startled Keegan into movement. He felt himself walking in a trance.

'It is a bit of a shocker,' said Bromley. 'Now I didn't want the gentleman to suffer like that, but Mr Graves was adamant. He always is. Keep moving. The door on the right.' They came to a passageway. 'But Mr Graves can be very generous. You won't have Viney to worry about any more. Do this job well and you're in the clear, Keegan.'

Gradually Keegan recovered. He had seen the results of violence before. Third Division soccer wasn't for the timid. There had been the bursts of savagery in his club days. Viney was a vicious enemy, a killer if rumour was to be believed; but Keegan had taken no part in Viney's gangland battles. In gaol, Keegan had seen desperate encounters, but there was rarely serious injury. Never calculated butchery.

No wonder Viney was co-operative.

Bromley knocked on an ornate, highly polished door.

'Enter!' called a high-pitched voice.

No one pushed Keegan. Both men stood back to let him go forward. Nider let him see the cosh again. Keegan had made such gestures in his time to dissuade the teenagers who thought they might have a try, just this once. It had usually been enough. It was this time. Keegan knew he was still suffering from the beating: and Nider was ready.

He moved forward.

It was an office. A small man, almost tiny, was dwarfed by an enormous desk. Desk and man were ancient.

'Keegan, sir,' said Bromley.

Keegan thought: This is what scares Viney.

Flat black eyes unblinkingly regarded Keegan. The wrinkled grey skin of his face and hands had no sheen. Keegan thought of a drowned woman he had seen, an old drunken woman who had fallen into a canal. The police had been careless with the blanket. He had hurried Ruthie past the scene, but he had seen the skin. Dead. Like this creature's skin.

'This is Mr Graves, Keegan.'

Keegan thought: What have I got into? This old bastard had a man chopped into pieces. *What in God's name am I into? What kind of mob is it?*

Graves' skinny hand flapped, grey and loose-jointed. 'I want you to listen carefully, Keegan, because what I have to say I shall say just once.'

31

Keegan concentrated. The man sounded bored. It was the drawling voice of one of the Oxford and Cambridge poofs you hear on television and radio – slow, bored and contemptuous, utterly sure of themselves.

'You've been selected to join my organization temporarily because you owe money and you've no choice. I know about your debt to this small-time gangster you used to work for, and I know your qualifications for the task I have in mind. You will drive a container-vehicle back to Britain. Do it well, and you have a clear five thousand pounds in cash.' Keegan waited for him to mention the appalling photographs. 'You will be flown to Brussels. Your assignment is simple. You are taking over from another driver, who's unfortunately fallen ill. It's a type of vehicle you are familiar with. Your route is prepared, and Bromley will tell you exactly what to do. One more thing.'

Keegan saw the slight frown on the wrinkled head. It didn't indicate worry, more the consideration a toad might give a worm.

'You'll be picked up by a young woman just outside Brussels. She's expecting the other driver, not you. Her name is Cynthia Haydon, not a nice girl. Is she, Anthony?'

'No, Mr Graves.'

Keegan didn't think it necessary to comment. The weird black eyes hadn't blinked, not once.

'You'll treat her as you'd treat any other road-whore, Keegan. Be persuaded. Bring her with you. Fall in with her suggestions. From the look of you, you won't find it difficult.'

Now he was expected to say something.

'When do I get back, sir?'

'Sunday night,' said Bromley. 'I'll pick you up myself.'

Graves' thin lips trembled into a smile.

'Don't let us down, eh, Keegan?'

Keegan couldn't have spoken. There was an indescribable menace in the grey face. Dread filled him. He had thought of trying to slip away at some stage during the journey to the airport. He wouldn't. No. Who would look after Ruthie if these sadistic mobsters decided he didn't meet their requirements?

'Chop chop,' said Bromley. 'Move, move.'

Keegan felt worse when he saw he was to travel by executive jet. It was that important to the man called Graves.

It was a small blue and white plane, six-seater, ready to move off when the Mercedes slid to a stop. All the way to the airport Bromley had been giving him instructions.

'It's a Leyland articulated vehicle they tell me,' he said. 'Driver and vehicle on hire. You'll find all the necessary documents in a compartment underneath the dash. They've been checked over. Here's your own licence and passport.' He passed a wallet. 'Money. French, Belgian, British. You won't need more. The fuel tanks are full. You sleep overnight *there*.' Bromley showed him the route-map. 'Bed down in the cab. The girl too. Tell her you can't afford a bed.'

'Why?'

'To make it look good. You're carrying a valuable load.'

Keegan was recovering fast now.

'Is she one of your lot?'

Behind him, Keegan heard Nider giggling softly.

'She's what you might call the opposition,' said Bromley. 'She won't bother you.'

Keegan was very confused.

'I don't get it.'

Bromley sped into the fast lane.

'You don't have to. Be surly. Don't answer questions too readily. But let her see you can be led. She's there to see that the load doesn't reach its original destination.'

'A hijack?'

It was making some kind of sense.

'More or less.'

'You want it done?'

'Good good!'

Bromley was smiling, white teeth, a heavy tan.

'And what happens to me?'

'You'll not be involved. Just go along with what you're told. Act scared.'

'What if something goes wrong. How do I get in touch?'

Bromley didn't answer for a while. 'Don't think of it.' They had taken extreme precautions. The harness again, a soft, black hood that muffled the sound and blanked off all light. The big Merc winding in and out of side-streets for half an hour. No possible chance of locating the house. 'We'll know, Keegan.'

Keegan wanted to ask questions. The most pressing was: Why me? Instead he said:

'How do I get the money?'

'In the post.'

'When?'

'Tuesday.'

It could be twenty Pakkies paying a thousand pounds each for a share in the Welfare State. It could be drugs. Even butter. Butter-smuggling was big business inside the Common Market. But you didn't chop a man in pieces for butter. Drugs? Then why a container-lorry.

Keegan played it just dumb enough.

'If it's twenty-odd Pakkies stuffed in there, I don't want to be on a murder charge. What if there's a hold-up? Accidents happen.'

'There'll be someone around.'

It got worse the more you thought about it. Anyone who could make so many complex arrangements at short notice could find a bent driver willing to drive a rig halfway to Hell for that kind of money. There was no need to show the horror photos.

'And I'll be back Sunday?'

'I'll pick you up personally.'

'Sure?'

'And paid on Tuesday. Isn't that nice?'

Bromley led the way to the aircraft.

Over the whine of the jets he said:

'Just think of it as another job, Keegan. By the way, do you know what upset our last guest more than anything?'

Keegan didn't want to hear the macabre details. 'When Nider—' and, thank God, it was lost in the roar of exhausts '—and have a good trip, Keegan!'

As the little plane bustled into the air, Keegan let out a long sigh. It wasn't relief.

The flight was too short.

There was little fuss at the airport. The pilot, a youngish long-haired character, said little, but he knew what to do, where to go, what to say. The language came easily to his lips, yet not a word came through to Keegan except when he gave Keegan his name. *Keegan.* The way he said it, it sounded like someone else. A machine to be pointed and set in motion. Graves' people were hard, competent, certain he'd do what they said. Keegan thought: My Christ, what do I do to get out of it? If it wasn't for Ruthie, he could hit this long-haired bastard hard and run for it, chance getting out of the airport and a lift back.

'Good-Good explained about the pick-up?' asked the young man.

Keegan didn't have to think for long. Nickname. *Good-good.* Bromley.

'No.'

'Change of plan. I put you in a cab. You don't get me.'

'Why—'

'One thing I learned soon. Never ask questions. They always lie to you.'

Keegan wondered if the youth was soft.

'Been with Graves' mob long?'

'Who's Graves?'

'Bromley's boss.'

'Him I wouldn't want to know. Bromley's bad enough. As for that flat-faced moron with him, he scares the life out of me.'

The airport wasn't busy. Not this corner of it, where the dusty Peugeots and Saabs and Simcas were parked. He was a slight young man. He'd cave in after a few good kicks. Keegan wondered about it.

But the pilot was ahead of him.

'Cab there.' He beckoned and the grimy Renault wheeled like a gundog. 'Mr Graves said you might want this.' He handed over the parcel. It was light, about the size of a shoe-box. Keegan waited and the pilot gave the cab-driver instructions. More gibberish, and money changed hands.

There was no farewell. The pilot turned away and Keegan found himself whizzing through streets that could have been Liverpool or London or Lille. Anywhere in Europe.

Keegan put the parcel on the seat and looked past the thick neck of the driver. He thought of Graves, then Viney.

Without any kind of conscious deduction, he suddenly realized that Viney had been setting him up for years. After the year in gaol Keegan couldn't get a regular job driving. Viney had been on hand, smiles and murmured commiserations at his bad luck, offering the loan.

Keegan glanced down at the parcel. The word had gone out for a bent driver, and he had been offered. The job stank of betrayal. Viney knew what he was doing sending him to Graves.

Suddenly, the parcel itself became part of the menace, part of the set-up. Keegan grabbed it and ripped away the Sellotape. It was a shoe-box after all. He flicked off the lid.

His soundless roar burst inside his head.

He stared at the doll, not believing what he saw.

Packed in cotton-wool, the thing was an obscenity.

Ruthie's doll. *Miss May*, she called it, the doll he had bought two years ago for her birthday. Plastic, a none-too-clean yellow dress, it was all he could afford and yet she adored it. She took it everywhere.

Mutilated. Butchered.

The hands and feet had been sliced off, the eyes gouged out, the dress slashed, the smooth plastic navel burned.

Miss May. Ruthie.

Keegan could not breathe. The collar of his shirt bulged. His eyes misted red, all the muscles of his upper body ridged stone-hard. Rage and then a cold seeping dread left him in a voiceless anguish.

Keegan shut his eyes against the sight.

Graves. Graves and the slope-shouldered, half-smiling beast. The terrible photographs they had shown him. Ruthie's doll. *Ruthie!!*

Keegan gasped, half-strangled by crazed rage. He had not realized the cab had stopped. The pig-faced taxi-driver was waving to him, hand open. Gibberish rattled around the cab.

They were at a transport halt. A rig started up. Its burnished metal dazzled Keegan. He looked again at Miss May. Slashed. Vilely burned. What kind of animal could *think* of doing that to a child? Because that was what Graves was saying. It was a reminder of the venomous assurance of the man.

In the morning sunlight, Keegan's rage faded.

The taxi-driver was bawling now. Keegan moved. He thought of Ruthie. She wouldn't give up Miss May without a struggle. So there had been a struggle.

They were sure of themselves, Graves' mob. Swift, cruel, and diabolically sure of themselves. They had found Ruthie without any trouble.

The taxi-driver opened the door and yelled at Keegan. Keegan closed the shoe-box, hiding the torn plastic body. He got out of the cab.

The driver held his hand out, still yelling.

Keegan heard him. Gibberish. He looked down, puzzled, into the fat red face. He felt a jab in his stomach. The driver's hand, open, demanding. Money, Keegan guessed. But he had been paid. And, anyway, the insane nasal gibberish coming from his wet lips affronted Keegan, for this was a moment when he had to hold on to himself, or he would shout his rage and anguish and dread to the world: and snap. And then what would become of Ruthie?

Keegan took the open hand. It wasn't big. Fat, over-fleshed. He tightened his grip and stared at the man's small eyes. He remembered a word of French, a lorry-driver's term:

'Merde!'

The driver opened his mouth again; and saw the inhuman rage in Keegan's eyes. Keegan let the hand drop. The man backed away, spitting out threats, waving his arms, but without any confidence. He had seen enough of violence, to know Keegan's state of mind. *Sale Anglais!*

Keegan forgot him.

For several moments he was obsessed by one thought: Ruthie would want another doll just like Miss May. Then he felt the ice-cold douche of dread. Viney had been much too satisfied with himself.

He wasn't meant to see Ruthie again. Nothing could be more certain. Keegan's eyes filled with tears. They sprang in a shining flood and trickled down his high cheekbones, a lifetime's regret in the wet stream. A pair of lorry-men, small, dark-haired, broad-shouldered drivers, were staring at him from the shade of a Crane Fruehauf artic. On the three-lane motorway, traffic whined and shrilled towards the coast.

37

He had to control himself. There was nothing he could do, nothing. Viney had won. The London mobsters had him tight. There was nothing he could do but follow orders. The mutilated doll was a warning.

Keegan tucked the box under his arm feeling that he carried a coffin. He walked towards the garishly painted rig, too stupefied, too appalled by what he could see of the future, to begin to think of fighting back.

It was the worst moment of his life.

Nothing could equal it, not Tina's yells of glee when she told him she'd been to bed with Viney even when she'd been carrying Ruthie; not the bitter mid-afternoon when the cell-door clanged on him and he knew that, whatever remission he gained, he would be in the hate-filled, stinking prison for a year; not even the sick realization that Viney's goons were going for him and that he had to let them beat him. None of these things remotely approached the dead and dumb anguish that filled him.

Keegan stared up at the cab door for a full minute. Then he climbed in.

'I suppose you don't mind some female company, do you, sweetie?'

She hardly impinged on Keegan's consciousness.

'What?'

He had an impression of slim legs, the usual lank hair to the waist, cornflower-blue eyes, and another of those well-bred, over-educated, over-privileged upper-class voices. Keegan groped for memories. This was important. A woman. He tried to focus his unhinged, scrambled, leaping thoughts on her.

She sighed.

'I saw the Merseyliner flash,' she said. 'I want a lift. What's the matter with you – too much booze?' She looked closer. Keegan saw how startlingly blue her eyes were. 'Been in a punch-up? A bit of Belgian bird, was it? Possessive sods, down here.'

Keegan still clutched the shoe-box.

'What's that? Sandwiches? Mind if—'

She reached to take it. Keegan's big hand slammed down. The girl yelped.

'I only asked! Shit, you didn't have to do that! I can buy my own nosh. All I want is a lift somewhere near the Pool.'

Keegan saw the fading white patch on her thin, bronzed arm where he had hit her. For a moment he saw the frailness of Ruthie's limbs. He reached to her.

'You don't get any of that!' she yelled. 'No, you sadistic shit! No nookie for you mate!'

Keegan remembered now. *She'll approach you right away at the transport stopover.* Bromley had spelled it out clearly. *Don't encourage her, or she'll know something's wrong. Be as surly as you like. She'll know you're not the regular driver, but that's no reason to volunteer information.*

He looked at her. A face missing beauty through gauntness. Watering, bulbous eyes, brilliant blue. Older than he had conjectured. Nearer thirty than twenty. Graves knew her, so did Bromley. *Graves.* Keegan's thoughts drifted again. He looked at his hands. It would be nothing to snap the scrawny neck.

The woman saw the convulsive movement of his hands.

'Do we get to Dover today or don't we?'

Keegan could answer a question of fact.

'No.' And, because he was determined to do what Bromley had ordered, right down to the letter, he said gruffly: 'How do you know it's Dover this run?'

He'd show the right amount of caution. Keegan could trust his instincts now.

'See,' said the woman. She pointed to the papers beneath the dash.

Keegan pulled out the thick plastic wallet. All there: export note, import permit, universal Customs certificate, green card, route and loading points form, agency card for fuel, ferry tickets. He pretended to check them, knowing they'd be right.

'Cheeky cow!'

He wanted to hit back-handed at her, force her to tell him why she was there.

'What's your name?'

'Cynthia.'

'I'll take you.'

'I thought you would.'

Keegan smiled. It was a mockery of amusement, but it showed his teeth. There was a time when the girls at the club had whispered about Keegan's smile. Tiger-face, they'd called him. It was a life time ago, in a different world. Kids' stuff, kids' games, playground leftovers. He'd been set up by experts now. It came to Keegan that Graves must be a Syndicate front man. Who else could arrange things so surely?

So what was the woman for?

The Leyland was a good motor. Smooth and powerful, it rumbled gently like a great cat as he worked the gears. Keegan was half-hypnotized by its silky power. He liked driving. With the window down and a good road, he could almost begin to relax. He was conscious of the woman watching him.

She wanted to talk. Pick-up girls always did. But she wasn't the ordinary kind, she had a purpose in hitching a lift, she was part of the set-up.

Let her talk.

'I know what you're thinking,' she said. 'Keegan, isn't it? Terence Keegan. I know what you're thinking, Keegan,' she repeated, and Keegan could see the blue of her eyes deepening to violet in the reflection from the windscreen.

'You could make money.'

'Aren't you the clever sod! Quips from Keegan! But you're a yob, Keegan, aren't you? Just a truck-driving yob, up and down the motorways day in, day out. All you know about life is what you see on the road.'

Keegan could hear the hatred behind her words. It wasn't the ordinary sarcasm of the educated fool. He could recognize the authentic ring of suppressed violence. He knew it well.

'If you want to ride with me, don't bitch.'

She was silent for a few minutes. Her hands were tight clenched. Gradually, she relaxed. When she spoke she was in control of herself.

'Keegan, I don't need a lift. I can afford to travel any way I like. I choose to travel this way.' Keegan nodded. 'I'm finishing off a doctorate. Do you know what that is, Keegan?'

40

'You tell me.'

'I'm studying to be a Doctor of Philosophy. I'm a political economist.'.

'You can buy the meal tonight.'

That was the right line. No compromising. Stay the hard bastard.

'I know what you're thinking, and no smart answers, Keegan.' She waited, but Keegan didn't comment. 'You've thought about it and you think I'm easy, don't you? An easy lay. You've said to yourself: She's easy, she's a lorry-whore, she'll come across.' Keegan let her talk. She was breathing faster. 'You've said to yourself: She's seen the hair on my chest and she's sick with wanting it. Wet pussy, that's her, that's what you're saying, isn't it, Keegan?'

Keegan smiled. He hadn't heard the term before.

'You supercilious shit! Smile, but you won't get it! I'm not one of the lorry-slags you're used to. I'm not one of the dismal tarts that pass for women in the north, all fat tits and varicose veins.'

'You're all right.'

'You've been used to overweight cows with halitosis and flat feet, and now that you've come across a girl with a bit of breeding, you're set alight, aren't you?'

Keegan looked sideways. She had thin but well-shaped legs. Her thighs were muscular and brown. At another time, he would have taken what she offered. But she was in the set-up.

She explained how desirable she was as the engine throbbed and whined along the motorway. When he wouldn't answer, she told him about her studies (she was working on a mathematical theory he couldn't remotely understand). She said her father was a baronet, and, despite himself, Keegan was impressed. And she detailed Keegan's erotic state of mind until he was sick of her nervous chatter.

She was an intelligent fool.

'For Christ's sake,' he said, and he grabbed her thin neck and pushed her down to his crutch. She shrieked that he was a pervert, but she didn't struggle much, and after a minute or two her thin fingers began to search and she found what she needed, and then her bleak silly talk stopped.

41

Keegan felt defiled. Yet he had answered her greedy need to get the woman's co-operation.

After a while, Keegan detached her.

'You make me sick, Keegan!' she yelled. 'You should be castrated!'

She screamed and raved at him, bitter curses full of wild obscenity. Keegan listened hard for a clue to her reasons for picking him up; but there was nothing. He thought: Clever rotten cow. She could detach from her schemes and take her pleasure at will. And he would have to suffer her company all night. He jerked the thirty tons of the vehicle hard over with unnecessary power. Bromley wanted this: a stopover near Ypres.

'Why not go through to Dover tonight?' she asked.

'I'm ahead of schedule. Anyway I want some sleep.'

The woman sneered, excitement and violence chasing across her thin features.

Bromley took the call from Brussels.

'On its way,' said Eichstatt. 'Your new boy was quite impressive. Cynthia's with him, drooling.'

'You tested the tracers?'

'Yes. I guarantee them. They're Russian. Very good.'

'Good good. The driver?'

'He won't be talking for a week or two. That enough?'

'Two days should do it.'

'I wouldn't like to be your new driver.'

'He's unimportant.'

'His bad luck.'

Both men rang off.

Bromley reported to Graves at once.

'It seems to be going quite nicely,' he said. 'Keegan's with the Honourable Cynthia and she's quite taken with him. A good choice, sir. Our man in Brussels had plenty of time to test the little specials. The load will reach Dover at about eleven Sunday morning, then, say eight, nine hours to the off-loading depot.'

Graves, flat forehead came up from his desk.

'Use that newspaper fellow you know to pass on the news to the Provisionals.'

'Rankin, sir.'

'Yes.'

'It'll take time to relay the news to the Belfast H.Q., sir, so I arranged for Keegan to stay overnight in Belgium. It gives them enough time to fix an interception.'

'Good. Make it tempting. You know the form. Keegan's a part-timer for the Special Branch – like that laddie they found last week with two bullets in his head.'

'They'll try to make him talk.'

'What can he tell them? Only that he was hired to drive a lorry, Anthony. And when they ask him who hired him, they're not going to believe he doesn't know, of course, so where will Keegan end up?'

Bromley smiled.

'It saves Nider some cleaning up.'

'How about liaison with our Army friends?'

'I've done that already, sir.'

Graves didn't look content, nevertheless his tone was approving:

'A neat little operation, Anthony. Apart from the unpleasantness with the child. Nider should have been more careful. Don't like children mixed up in these things. The wrong people hear about it, then they get emotional. How is she?'

Bromley wasn't interested.

'I think she'll live.'

'Witnesses?'

'We weren't that stupid, sir.'

'Then that's all right.' Graves' obsidian eyes gleamed wet. 'Tell Nider to get the sauna ready. I feel like a little relaxation.'

Bromley hid his distaste.

'Yes, sir.'

The lorry park was an immense area, stretching half a mile back from the service station. Scores of huge rigs gleamed under the yellow arc-lamps. It was new, open only a year or two, but it was already dilapidated. When Keegan cut the engine, he could smell the tainted air: diesel fumes, hot burned fat from the cafes, bad drains. Music blasted from a dozen points in the complex of one-storey concrete buildings. Keegan saw women lounging beside one of the cafes. It looked as though the place had its prostitutes.

'You can buy the food,' said Keegan.

The woman shrugged.

'I buy the steaks, you pay for the beds.'

'I sleep in the cab.'

'Christ!'

'Company orders.'

Bromley had been insistent. The woman would know the rule. It was against U.K. regulations for a driver to bed down in his cab, but not many international companies would let a load out if the driver didn't keep to his vehicle.

Over the meal, the woman began to question him.

'How long have you been on this run, Keegan?'

'My first with this company.'

'Oh?'

She was a curious and intelligent bitch, very alert. For all her greedy lusting, she was a danger.

'I do relief crew for an agency. One-off jobs. I go anywhere.'

Tell her so much, Bromley had said. Enough to satisfy a normal curiosity, no more.

'Better than regular turns?'

Keegan got up.

'You're a nosey cow, aren't you?' He walked away. The woman paid the bill and followed. A Spaniard called to her. She couldn't resist smiling back at him.

'Keegan!'

He walked on.

'All right, sod you!'

She wasn't following any more. Keegan felt icy sweat under his shirt. The cow had turned, gone back to the cafe. He almost followed her. She was the one thread he could pull on. The only lead he had to the evil little bastard in London. Keegan heard her call to the Spaniard. She sounded fluent.

Bromley's words came to him. In his drawling, over-confident and bored voice, he had foreseen such an eventuality. 'She's a temperamental nymphomaniac,' Bromley had

44

drawled. 'Don't let it worry you if she behaves oddly. It's her job to stick by you all the way to Liverpool. Be cool, Keegan, if you want to be able to keep your side of the bargain.'

At that time, it had been a bargain for five thousand pounds. Not for Ruthie.

As he neared the gleaming Leyland, a shortish middle-aged man brushed against Keegan. It was done with the minimum of fuss. He looked like a lorry driver, apologized in French, and was away before Keegan realized that the message was in his hand. Keegan ran, but other drivers were drifting about the lorry-park. In the harsh light and deep shadows any one of the drivers could be the right one. It was futile to follow.

He read it in the cab, a pencil scrawl on a stained menu from the cafe where he had just eaten. Keegan's mind raced. He hadn't seen the man at the cafe. But he had been there.

'Good so far,' he read. 'Leave on schedule in the morning. Don't worry about a thing. You'll see R. tomorrow.'

Bile rose in Keegan's throat. The garlic-rubbed steak grated in his guts. He saw his reflection and then he had to look away for it showed utter despair.

They had taken her. When? Before Viney's mob came to the house? In the night? In the silent dawn, breaking in on pig-drunk Auntie Edie and bundling Ruthie's thin, sleep-washed frame down to the waiting Merc all in a couple of minutes.

Or had Viney been given the job?

There was nothing, nothing at all, he could do. Except vow vengeance. For every second that Ruthie had suffered fear and terror, there would be an accounting.

Hours later Keegan's despair had burned itself out, and sleep came. The short night passed in broken dreams. With the grey dawn, there was the draught of cold air and a man's gruff snort of amusement. Keegan gulped into consciousness.

'Awake, Keegan?' asked the woman.

'Who was with you?'

He could just see her face, taut with a strange triumph. 'Someone a bit more active than you, sweetie.' She thrust her hands into the side-pockets and began to pull out handfuls of

45

notes. 'I'll say this for the members of your profession, Keegan. They may be sweaty, but they pay.'

Keegan saw crumpled notes of different currencies. The woman had been on the game. She was staring at his face expectantly. What did she want? A backhander across the face? Sex again? Both?

Her eyes gleamed. There was a mad look about her that reminded Keegan of a woman who had lost heavily at roulette at Viney's club. She'd had the same expression: a sick, triumphant and fulfilled self-abasement. Keegan told her what she wanted to hear.

'You're a dirty cow, aren't you?'

She began to revile him. He wasn't a man at all, just a pervert who couldn't do it the normal way. He had forced her into associating with greasy Spaniards and brutal Germans. He played it her way.

'If you're so stinking rich, you pay for your ride. All the meals from now on. All right?'

'You're even sicker than I thought, Keegan! You'd let a girl pay for you out of what she takes on the game? Would you?'

Keegan pushed her away.

'Pay or don't ride to Liverpool. You've enough there to fly first-class. And don't wave your fanny at me. I wouldn't touch you if you boiled it in Harpic.'

She wouldn't join him for breakfast, so Keegan sipped the strong sweet coffee alone. A couple of German drivers looked at him curiously, but they said nothing. Keegan bought aspirin. The bruises were red and blue on his ribs, and his leg was giving trouble. That was the way with collision injuries. Two days to show, then another two to heal.

Keegan didn't stop again. The woman sulked in silence. Keegan waited till she was slumped in a deep sleep. Her battered leather satchel wasn't fastened.

He sorted through it and found her passport. It was fairly new, which surprised him. Her name was Cynthia Haydon, place of birth, Poole. She was five feet seven in height, hair black, eyes blue. In the passport photograph she was much younger, but the hard lines were already deep-grooved, the eyes challenging. There were stamped entries for a dozen

46

European countries. She had been to Egypt, Syria and Tunisia in the past few months. Keegan looked at her caked make-up and the grime-rimmed ears. She needed sex the way some women needed gossip, a clever and well-educated bitch. What was her tie-up with Graves and his mob?

He fumbled through her few possessions. A couple of packs of cigarettes. He examined the opened pack. Just cigarettes, black tobacco, French. There was no purse or wallet, no underclothes, no letters. She had a pair of flimsy sandals, much worn, and a sweater, nothing to point to the nature of her employers or her reason for picking him up.

He lit one of his own cigarettes. The lorry sang smoothly. Little French cars buzzed close, hooting for road-room. The shriek of a police-car sounded behind him. Trouble, but well behind him. *The police.* Keegan ground the cigarette into the ash-tray. What use would it be to go to the police? They'd check. The record would be there. G.B.H. Grievous Bodily Harm. The pink faces would be amused. A hard man like him running to the law. Keegan's hands were tight on the wheel.

He was still gripping the wheel too hard an hour later when the girl awoke. She blinked and watched him. Keegan sensed her tension.

'I don't have to hitch, Keegan,' she said, and her voice still had that edge of irritated dissatisfaction. 'I'm not a slag.'

Later, she wanted to stop, so they had a hamburger and coffee. She paid without prompting.

'I'm studying economic growth,' she told him. 'But you wouldn't know what that was, would you, Keegan. High-powered research, Keegan, at the London School of Economics. I don't make a habit of taking up with your kind, Keegan. When I do, it's strictly for my own amusement. Sometimes I like to dabble in the dirt.'

Keegan said nothing. She was an over-educated female version of Graves and Bromley. Their kind never worked. You found them in any job where they could sit on their backsides all day and give orders. Keegan held back his anger. He had to wait for her to make her move. There would be one.

And then it would lead back to Graves.

They reached the Dunkirk ferry at eleven. Four hours later they were in Dover.

The crossing was uneventful. Keegan spent most of his time on deck savouring the crisp cool sea air. He had taken Ruthie to the seaside when a run allowed it, which wasn't often. The school came first. If she was frequently absent, there would be questions and then the visits from the inquisitive Welfare bitches. Backing them was the court. Keegan leant over the side and watched the waves. The care order could still be altered. He hung on to his sick fury by the exercise of the self-control he had learnt during the grey months of gaol.

There was no way of stopping the bastards with the power, none. So you waited and didn't offer offence, you didn't challenge them if you couldn't beat them. Keegan knew he couldn't risk it, not yet. The cost of failure was too high.

The woman recognized his mood and kept away. Keegan barely noticed her absence. She was peripheral, Ruthie the reality.

Through the protracted inspection of carnets, seals, licences, inventories, and then a snap check on emergency brakes at Dover, Keegan kept down his bitter impatience. He managed a smile at a Customs official's lewd inquiry about the woman. Then another Customs official banged on the container and yelled, 'Are you all right in there?' Keegan laughed at the old joke which wasn't funny since the Pakkies entering illegally a few months ago had shouted, 'Oh yes, thank you, are we in Birmingham now?' He saw a driver who recognized him from seven years back and spoke to him about motorway halts. He didn't mention Keegan's long absence from the roads. All very normal and low-key.

Keegan sent the woman to the pierside cafè. He spoke to her as she expected, brusque, uncouth. She returned looking tired. She had bought a paperback with a blue cover. Keegan caught part of a word he didn't know.

He drove just inside the limit along the motorways. A new junction aroused his attention, but otherwise it was just another haul. He had made hundreds of such journeys in his twenties. Service station after service station, countryside the same for long spells, with the corn mostly cut and the sun glaring from a blue sky. If he hadn't met Viney that night, eight, nearly nine years back, this would have been his life. But he had. And Viney's offer was too good to turn down. 'You're big and tough, but not hard-looking, Terry.' The years rolled back. 'You won't have much trouble. Lots of our customers know you. They like you. And you can handle the few yobs who want trouble. It pays a lot better than driving.' It had. For a while. Then Tina, false thin-boned Tina, heavy with Ruthie and laughing at his bemused shame. Then the bad years. Now, the worst of all. Keegan thought about Graves, and Nider. Nider, with his expres-sionless eyes and wide fat hands. Keegan imagined those hands on Ruthie. Momentarily he closed his eyes, appalled.

'Keegan, watch out!'

The Sunday driver pulled the little Ford directly into his line. He braked, not too sharply, almost sweeping into the bright red car with its head-wagging dog and three delighted young kids on the back seat.

'Christ!'

'You fell asleep!' she yelled. 'You nearly wiped out the whole bloody family! Keep your eyes on the road!'

Commands. Keegan almost side-swiped her. Any other woman he would. He held back. She hadn't said she wouldn't ride any further. She was in it, and there was a way to Graves, a way out of the mess. He had to believe it.

'I didn't sleep much.' He was being too humble. 'You keep your great mouth shut from now on!'

It wasn't a pleasant journey.

Keegan felt fatigue gum on his eyelids. Liverpool was sixty-eight miles away, so the signpost said. It was early evening. Ruthie had been away from the only person who cared about her for anything up to twenty-four hours. Keegan's head roared. He thought: I have to take it. *Anything*.

He waited for the thin, hard voice, willing her to speak. Half an hour passed. The speedometer remained steady at sixty-eight, dipped to sixty-five, then sixty as they climbed.

The gears slid in easily, silken, a beautiful engine, eight sweet gears.

She was clever about it. Later he knew he was no match for her. She put her thin hand on his arm and squeezed.

'I've been rather a rotten sort of cow, haven't I, Keegan.' Then, charmingly, 'Terry?'

He cleared his throat. Whatever she said.

'As you said, love. You're not the usual sort.'

'I was wondering—' and he couldn't say I think you're in the set-up, Graves' woman, a treacherous cow with no mercy, no morals, no honesty. The words stuck. A barrier he could recognize but not define stood solidly between the harsh words and his ability to say them.

'Look, we did have a bit of fun, didn't we? I mean, I know I'm not your kind, Terry, but it wasn't so bad, was it?'

'I've had worse.'

'So you wouldn't mind doing me a favour?'

Here it came: *Don't rush it.* 'What?'

'Drop me somewhere near home.'

'Where's that?'

'About eight miles off the next junction. It won't take you much out of your way. Not more than half an hour.'

'It'll cost you.'

'How much?'

'A fiver.'

'Terry!'

'You said you were well-off.'

'All right. A fiver.'

'Before I turn off.'

She smiled affectionately. Her eyes were brilliant, blue stones underwater, the lights dancing with a strange excitement. She pushed a five-pound note into his waistband.

'Are you sure that's all you want?' she asked as the great vehicle took the A road.

'I'm due with this load.'

Sex with her. Keegan could have vomited.

'We'll see, shall we?'

He followed her directions. She wanted the North Wales road. It wouldn't take long. Sunday motorists hooted behind him, furious as the huge vehicle whined up hills.

50

'Terry, you're rather a nice person, really,' she said. 'I wish we'd got to know one another a bit better. I could give you my phone number in case you're ever in these parts?'

She played it cleverly. An ordinary young woman now, not brash and aggressive, the grating edge gone from her voice. Keegan was wary. Yet the first move caught him unawares. Because he was concentrating, or because he was tired, or because Ruthie's thin face kept swimming before him. And his leg hurt. It had held down the heavy lever for the whole of the day. The ligaments creaked, a nagging pain. He was tense, tired, irritable. Not careful at all.

'Down there,' she said, and Keegan, listening for the trap, fell into it. He hadn't checked the signpost, couldn't check it now, for he had automatically signalled and there was a line of traffic behind him, and he was clear in the opposite lane. 'It's the back road to the village,' she said. 'You drop me and then you take the Chester road out, and you're back on the Liverpool road right away. About another mile, Terry. Did you want my home number? Shall I write it down?'

'Yes,' said Keegan.

She searched for a pen. She smiled. 'No pen!' Then she saw the wallet of documents with the pen clipped to the back.

She wrote carefully, then she looked up, a sweet, clever, smiling girl:

'Oh, sod it, Terry, can you stop? It was the lane back there – it leads to our place.'

Keegan slowed. He was expecting anything but what happened. An accident with a fake casualty would not have impressed him, nor a police stop. If a private motorist had flagged him down, he would have known the wheel in the road wasn't punctured. The sheer brutality of it caught him.

He was stopping the vehicle when the old Dodge came out of the farm track. Keegan braked. There was nothing else to do. He heard the tyres of the Leyland screaming, saw black smoke, then a thin dark face intently staring at the front of the Leyland, judging distances, calculating, and then the eyes turned on Keegan in a crazy glare.

Keegan was already trying for reverse gear when the Dodge hit. The artic juddered, the Dodge slewed sideways. The girl reached across, tearing at the ignition. Keegan

51

slammed her sideways, but he had lost seconds. He was vaguely aware of hooded men scrambling towards him, swarming up the sides of the cab, steel bars dully swinging, then the smashing of glass. The woman was screaming, holding her mouth. Blood ran. The Leyland's engine boomed. Keegan managed to engage reverse gear, but a bar smashed on to his shoulder and suddenly there was the black menace of an automatic pistol in his face.

'Stop the engine!' screamed a voice, high and young, Liverpool–Irish adenoidal, full of terror and suicidal menace.

Keegan reached out. A bar hovered. The automatic shook; at a range of two feet he couldn't miss. Keegan switched off the engine. Already there was the sound of a sledge-hammer at the back.

'Out.'

'You mad—'

Keegan saw the bar coming straight for his face. He dived to the side.

'Out and shut yuh fuckin' gub!' screamed the hyper-excited Liverpool–Irish youth.

Keegan scrambled out of the cab. The woman was yelling something behind him, a piercing obscene screaming. Gall ran into his veins, furious grief and rage. *Irish.* It didn't take much thinking out now. Bog-Irish with guns.

Keegan heard the thick hoarse voices. Several of them – not comic Micks, the other kind, the deadly, obsessed ambushers, those who tortured before they killed. He roared silently: *Why me mixed up in this!*

He heard the slam-slam of the sledge-hammer and then tearing metal. The cargo. What was it – guns? Armalites? Grenades? And why Graves mixed up in it? Surely the mobs didn't mix with the Provisionals?

'Move!' growled an older man. Keegan saw a faded blue suit and dusty black shoes, a close-fitting stocking mask, through it dark eyes fixed on him, and another of those dull-black automatics.

'Wait, Sean!' screamed the woman. She was jumping from the cab, underwear showing, a wolverine grimace on her face, blood running from split lips.

'For what?'

'This!'

She launched herself at Keegan, nails raking. Keegan shifted sideways. She missed and lurched on to the tarmac, screaming again.

'Leave be, what's the fuck's got into yez?'

'He hit me – the bastard *hit* me!'

'You soft in the head? You know we've got no time now – keep away!' To the excited youth he shouted:

'Away, Kev, help round the back!'

Keegan waited for the moment when the gun would look away from him. The barrel never wavered. He would shoot at a hint of movement.

The woman was still raging. Her eyes lit on an iron bar, discarded now. She went to it, needing two hands to pick it up.

'Stand away, Sean. Let me smash the big bastard!'

'Away!' he snarled.

'Go with Kev – away and help with the launchers.'

Launchers. Keegan registered the word. Rocket-launchers. The latest addition to the terrorists' armoury, light-weight and devastating. So the load had been arms.

'Promise you'll let me have him for a minute before you turn him loose, Sean?'

She was colder and calmer, her blue eyes gleaming murder.

'Who said anything about turning him loose?'

'Look, I'm just a driver—'

A ridiculous memory came from somewhere. An Irish joke: 'Did you hear about the Irishman who wanted to test the air-brakes of his truck? Drove it over a cliff . . .!' *Irish jokes.* Once they had been nig jokes, after that, the Pakkies. Not at all funny.

'Shut yer gub!' The automatic was fixed on Keegan's shirt. He looked down and saw the blood. The woman's, where she had sprayed over him. The woman looked puzzled. 'He doesn't get away, the dirty informer!' growled Sean. 'Fuckin' S.I.B. spy! Now, away, Cyn!'

'Sean!' bellowed someone. 'Back here – bring the driver. We're in a hurry!'

53

Sean motioned. Keegan moved carefully. His right knee quivered. He thought: He said *informer*. Me.

There were three more of them, all busy unstacking heavy boxes. One of them turned, the thin young gunman who had first threatened him:

'Work, and put yer back into it, boyo, or you get it here and now – through the knees and belly before we put two in yuh fuckin' head!'

Keegan knew the state of murderous elation that held the Irishmen. It happened sometimes in gaol when a prisoner nursed a grievance through days and hours, months and years, until he fixed it on someone – prisoner or guard – and awaited the moment of release. A blaze of exultant violence. Nothing else mattered. Men distilled the venomous rage until in the whole world nothing mattered but its release.

Now these gunmen were singing with terrified, desperate, exultant rage. The youth dearly wished to pull the trigger.

Keegan staggered as Sean jabbed him in the kidneys.

'You're a big strong boyo,' Sean growled. 'Work – and put yer fuckin' back into it!'

S.I.B. they had called him. Keegan wasn't sure what it stood for, though it was police. The first word was *Special*. He didn't try to argue.

'Watch him, Cyn,' ordered Sean. He passed her yet another pistol. 'You at the front passing back,' he said to Keegan. 'Move.'

It took half an hour. Case after case of luxury tinned food, just as the manifest said. Keegan saw Dutch and French markings, heard the tins rattle softly. Behind him, the line sweated. *S.I.B.?* Special. *Investigation. Inquiry.* A police department, something like that. Keegan read the papers only occasionally, but there were the news broadcasts.

He was sick with angry fear.

Two bullets in the back of the head. *S.I.B.* Graves. The woman, with her endless chatter and brainy nonsense and her strange, mad eyes. She was with them, these gun-crazy Irish. With a load of rockets. *What do you call an Irishman who can count up to 10?* Keegan began to remember more of the unfunny jokes. Anyway, what did you call an Irishman who could . . .

'Faster!' bawled Sean.

Keegan's shoulder throbbed. His right leg began to ache from the wrenching the previous night. He hadn't slept much, and nervous tension had kept him from eating much during the long drive North. He wished he could make more sense of it. He felt like a bullock in a market-pen. The slaughterers waited.

He hefted a case weighing half a hundredweight and thought of bringing it down on the shoulders of the man next to him. The woman's cornflower eyes held him as he turned.

She would shoot, wanted to. He wondered what led to this lust for killing. *The Provisional I.R.A.* Ordinary men, so the newspapers said. Plasterers, postmen, construction workers, quite ordinary occupations: turned killer. Gun in hand, killing from ambush. *Liking it?*

For the first time in thirty minutes, Keegan remembered Ruthie. His back straightened.

He wanted to destroy at least one of the swine.

'There!' screamed the youth. 'Will yuh look! It's the rockets, Sean!'

The moment was gone, for they shouldered him away. Keegan had to throw the case aside to avoid wrenching his back. He looked too, for in an odd way he shared their interest. He had brought the rockets across half Europe.

He hadn't been forgotten.

'Back and away!' growled Sean. 'Cyn, if he moves, shoot him in the knees. She can,' he told Keegan. 'None better with the little gun. So watch it if you want to walk to your grave.'

Keegan knew they had killed before, all of them.

He moved carefully.

The unloading went forward quickly. Keegan saw yellow plastic packages three feet long, perhaps four inches wide, bulbous at one end, each with its carrying sling. They were not heavy. Hundreds. No one told him to help. A green one-tonner rolled forward from the cart-track, then a motor-cyclist reported to the thickset man called Sean.

Keegan caught some excited, hoarse words. 'Diversion ... trippers ... much longer.' A look-out. The motor-cyclist left in a hurry.

When the van was loaded, the thin-faced youth asked about Keegan.

'Do I shoot the dorrty spy now, Sean?'

Keegan flinched. This was the way it ended. A crash, the bullet slamming into his head. He saw the woman's mad eyes. He couldn't think of anything to say.

'No. Bring him. I want to know more about the bastards who set him on us.'

Keegan felt iron in his soul. This was the set-up. He looked from the wide cornflower-blue eyes of the woman. She needed sex, her eyes shone with lust.

'Hands behind your back,' one of the gang ordered. Through the mesh of the stocking Keegan saw a lumpy face. An ordinary man. Not tough-looking at all.

They tied him securely at the wrists and ankles and pushed him into the van, a gun at his head. There was a stop after a minute or so. Keegan heard Sean giving orders. The diversion signs down when the van was clear; Cynthia to telephone Brigade; Kevin, this the thin-faced youth, to keep an eye to the dirty British spy. Someone at the lane-end asked if the informer had been executed. Sean said no, that there were to be questions.

The van's engine boomed.

Keegan rolled hard against the metal sides, quite unable to protect himself. He thought: They mean it, Christ, they mean it! He tried to think of Ruthie, but she seemed to belong to another existence altogether. He was afraid but angry too, though the focus of his anger was not the uncouth fanatics who held him, nor Graves, nor even Nider. Keegan could think only of Viney's calculating expression.

Viney had started it, Viney knew the end result.

In his anguished confusion Keegan blamed all that had happened on Viney.

The drive lasted for a little over an hour, though Keegan had no way of telling what time had passed. He heard Sunday traffic, once the scream of brakes near a roundabout, and a train's two-tone yell. The bonds dug into him. There was no way of easing them, no give in the rope. After a while, the Liverpool-Irish youth ceased staring into his face and concentrated on the view from the back window.

Sean drove carefully and well. They were in no special hurry. Keegan remembered a radio report about an execution in Belfast. The I.R.A. had tortured a young lad for three days until they shot him. Keegan gritted his teeth against the cramp in his shoulders.

The van slid to a halt. Keegan glimpsed tall buildings. He thought they must be somewhere in Liverpool. Big doors rumbled. The van reversed and stopped.

They were expected. The van doors opened at once. Another two men were there. They were both big fellows in their thirties, hard men with those lumpy Irish faces and hands like grabs. *Dockers?*

'Is this the boyo?' asked one of the big men softly.

'That's the informer,' Sean told him.

Keegan couldn't avoid it. He was hauled like a stranded fish until he was on his knees. Then the big man who had asked the questions hit him solidly with his fist. Keegan felt cartilage crack. Blood began to pour. He snuffled, choking on the blood.

Sean ordered the beating to begin. 'Soften him,' he said, and then he turned away.

Keegan saw bare walls, a high space, blackened windows. He knew he was going to suffer, so he steeled himself. *Viney*, he thought as the blows began. Viney. Viney. *Viney*. There was no finesse about the torture. Balled fists on his chest, in his guts, his head and shoulders, nothing systematic about it. Both the men sweated by the time they beat him unconscious.

'Enough for now,' Sean ordered, when Keegan's head lolled on one side.

They didn't need to mount a guard, but they tied him in a sitting position to a ring-bolt on the wall. After that, they went into a glass-sided office and drank whisky until it was dark. Keegan regained consciousness three or four times, but slipped back into crazy, pain-soaked dreams afterwards. There was a pad between his teeth to keep him from suffocating on his own blood.

Shortly after midnight, there was a flurry of activity.

57

Keegan heard the noises distantly, without recognizing their meaning.

The woman was back with news. Trans-shipment of the rockets was under way. They would be in Belfast in the morning and distributed immediately. No slip-ups. So far, the police were treating the hi-jacking as an everyday crime. Sean listened and grinned, suddenly a much younger man.

'We'll blow a few dozen Brits up before the week's out. Jasus, Cyn, I'd give anything to be there when the boys get busy!'

'I talked to O'Halloran,' she said. 'He's pleased with the way we handled things, Sean. And he confirmed it was in order to interrogate the agent ourselves.'

Sean let his eyes fall on the slumped figure. 'We're going to shoot you, boyo,' he said. 'But not just yet.' He bent and turned the wrecked face upwards. Keegan's eyes remained closed.

'There's no hurry about him,' said the woman. 'Belfast said to keep him as long as necessary, learn what we could. He'll keep till morning, Sean.' She bent and let her tongue glide in his ear. 'It's been a while since I had a real man.'

Sean looked quickly at the office. A small oil-lamp glowed. There was a low hum of conversation.

'You'll want it in your coffin,' he said, amused. He put an arm round her thin waist and drew her into the shadows beyond Keegan.

Keegan, in his fourth or fifth moment of consciousness, heard the slight yelps and the soft noises of lust and thought they came from his own broken lips. When Sean laughed exultantly he smiled, thinking that he himself had seen the point of a good joke. *What did you call an Irishman . . .*

MONDAY

Morning and more pain.

Keegan had been lashed to an abandoned Victorian stool. In turn the stool was lashed to a bench in the office. Keegan opened his eyes. The thin-faced youth was back. He looked tired. Keegan's bladder troubled him. The pad was gone.

'You're going to talk,' Kevin assured him. 'You're going

to tell us all about the shitheads who sent you, Keegan. You stink, do you know!' he screamed. 'You stink rotten, you lump of English shit!'

Keegan wondered how he could endure the pain. It was so much worse now. Appalled, he made an inventory of its sources. Soccer taught you that the first thing you checked was for broken bones. He couldn't move more than an inch or two, so it took time. He thought his shoulder might be cracked. Ribs too. The right leg hadn't suffered too badly. There was a source of excruciating agony in the left hand. A finger wrenched back. There was a gap where three good teeth had been. From his upper belly came a complaint. He remembered an especially savage kick. Maybe a hernia.

Keegan tried to say something.

Kevin raked his skull with a chair-leg and Keegan waited for unconsciousness. Only dull aching pain followed. He opened his eyes. Viney's lot had been paid thugs. These fanatics loved their work.

He licked his lips. Blood clots moved. He needed a drink.

Kevin swung again and Keegan tried to push away.

'Stop!' roared Sean.

Keegan thanked him silently.

'Get some water,' he ordered. Kevin began to argue, but Sean glared until he left. Keegan heard water splashing. In sympathy, his bladder protested.

'Lavatory,' he croaked.

'Piss your pants.'

The water came. Kevin jerked the tin cup in his mouth. Keegan fouled himself as the water flooded his mouth. He couldn't swallow. Sean watched. He didn't care that Keegan examined his lined, young-old ruddy face with its small forehead and dangerous green eyes. He looked as if he trained. A fit, cruel bastard. Keegan thought: Those green eyes are the last thing I'll see. He knew it. He wished he could kick out just once. Sean saw the wish. He grinned, the devil-may-care dangerous Irish grin.

'Before we put a couple of bullets in your head youse'll talk,' he told Keegan. 'Get some water down him, Kevin. His mouth's full of last night's punishment. Swallow it.'

Keegan swallowed, thinking: They're maniacs. They come

59

over here and blow up people they've never met, they shoot down people they've never talked to; as if it's something at a fairground, tin cans falling down, screechy noises simulating missiles. And I'm the target. *How do I get out!*

The water washed the clots away.

'Who sent you?' snapped Sean when Keegan could feel gashes open, stinging.

Keegan wondered if some fanciful story would keep him alive long enough to have a hope of escape. Sean saw that too. He said quietly:

'Lie, and we'll break your bones one by one.'

'London mob,' croaked Keegan.

Sean nodded.

'Names?'

'Graves. Bromley.' He couldn't remember the other one. That was bad for the half-breed was the one he had to get hold of, the one who had handled Ruthie.

He missed the slight nod.

Kevin swung, not too far. Keegan heard a metallic sound in his left ear. For a moment, he didn't realize he had been hit. Then the sharp pain came.

'Names!'

'Nider,' said Keegan. 'Graves. Bromley. Nider.' He heard himself mouth the names, slurring and slipping the consonants like a foreigner.

Sean frowned.

'Who's the top man?'

'Graves.'

'Rank?'

Keegan was bewildered. He couldn't find an answer. He remembered Graves drawling something at him but not the words.

'Rank.'

The chair leg smashed down again. It hurt at once this time.

'He's the top man!'

'You're not very bright today, Keegan,' snarled Sean. He looked worried. Keegan placed his kind. He looked harder but somehow weaker without the mask. There were decent fellows amongst the Irish he knew, but this was a bad one.

The decent ones went quiet when the 'troubles' were mentioned in conversation. 'The name of this set of S.I.B. shits. Ranks. Strength and address. Now!'

'Speak up, you fuckin' spy!' screamed Kevin, very excited. Keegan noted the impatience of youth. The chairleg hovered. The youth had discovered that its broken end was sharp.

Keegan felt a great calmness come over him; he had endured the fear of Ruthie's loss and the dread of death. Undoubtedly they would kill him. Fear went. He didn't know why. He knew, however, that he could maintain some sort of presence. They believed that he was a police informer, a spy planted on them. But he had to try to live.

Before the blow came, he said: 'I thought they were a London firm. Syndicate, you know, American money backing them. I saw them just the once.'

Sean bent closer. His nose wrinkled in disgust.

'You're dead. But tell us what we want, and it'll be over quick. Otherwise, we've got days. Lots of days, Keegan. Now, do youse want it easy?'

Keegan felt a jagged tooth.

'I don't want it at all.' He felt his head swimming. 'I'm just a driver. Check, if you like. I've got a lorry. I shift limestone.'

'We're checking, don't fret,' said Sean. 'Who's Graves?'

'I told you. He hired me to drive the artic to Liverpool. He said the driver had gone sick.' Keegan saw the small eyes fill with distrust.

'We know you're an informer and a fuckin' spy,' Sean said coldly. 'Tell the rest of it while you've still got a mouth.'

'I was hired from Sheffield for the one trip.'

'When?'

'Friday night.'

'You've spied for the bastards before?'

'I'm not a spy! I was sent up to London by a fellow who's got me cold – I owe him money! I was to drive this one load and get clear of him. I'd never heard of Graves before—'

Again there must have been a sign.

The chair-leg was driven like a dart into the muscles at the left of his neck. It cut slowly, a tearing shallow wound. The two men waited for his reaction. Keegan restrained a yell of agony.

'Mind the artery,' warned Sean. 'Where did you see this Graves? Now some answers, boyo!'

'In London,' Keegan said. The pain wasn't bad, but he was losing a lot of blood. 'A big house.'

'Where?'

Keegan's own rage sprang out.

'I don't know! I was drugged.' But there was something, something he hadn't noticed at the time. Pain, fatigue, fear had forced the stray memory to the surface. He pushed it down, suddenly excited. Even though he had been half-unconscious, he had absorbed that *something*. His driver's instincts had been at work. But the memory was a blur, only a hint.

Sean motioned.

Kevin began to beat him. Keegan grunted and Sean held the excited youth back.

'Will you talk?' demanded Sean.

Keegan's mind was far away. The heavy brogue seemed to come from a distance. An Irishman, thought Keegan. *What do you call* . . .

'I'll count to ten, then he'll start,' Sean promised.

Keegan thought: *Count to ten?* Light blazed in his head. Of course! He knew what you called an Irishman who could count to ten.

'. . . six, seven. Eight. Nine. Ten,' finished Sean.

Keegan smiled at him.

'You must be a brain surgeon,' he said.

'He won't learn,' said Sean.

The Irishman turned his back, and blows rained down on Keegan's shoulders and arms. After a while, the pain stopped and a red flood engulfed him. Someone called harshly and that was all he knew.

MONDAY NIGHT

They had cut him free of the chair. Keegan lurched into consciousness. It was dark in the warehouse. He was aware of the passage of time. The day had passed. Tears of impotent anger trickled down his face. For the first time since the magistrate passed sentence he felt sorry for himself. How could one man hold out against the kind of sadistic bastards there were in the world?

He moved and found his bonds slacker. The cramps racked him and he had to roar out his anguish. Every time he moved, crushed bone and torn muscle shrieked. He closed his eyes as he heard light foot-steps.

'My, Keegan, you are a mess!'

It was Cynthia. The Honourable Cynthia Haydon. The intelligent cow. He looked up and tried to spit. Nothing came. Sean joined her. Keegan saw her strange eyes in the gloom. She rubbed against the Irishman's square shoulder.

'Ready to talk, Keegan?' said Sean. 'Have you had enough?'

Keegan nodded. The movement jerked the line of the gash in his shoulder. He wanted to kill the youth, but more than that he wanted to stand on his feet again, quite clean, just once.

'Where's Graves?'

Keegan mouthed 'London'. The woman smiled at him. She reached behind her and threw water into his face. Some of it splashed his lips. Keegan waited as she bent and let more liquid trickle into his mouth.

'London,' he said, hardly recognizing his voice. 'Not the centre. Blindfold.' He wanted to sink back into unconsciousness again.

'He's badly shocked,' he heard the woman say. 'Let me get some glucose down him. He's been out for hours. He needs food. I want him aware of what's happening. He's got to understand about the girl.'

Keegan heard the reference to 'the girl'. He tried to pretend he hadn't. There was only one girl they could be talking about. He didn't struggle when Sean took his head and the woman bathed his lips, nor when they gave him the sweet lemon-flavoured drink. Dread gripped him. Much worse.

Sean took up the questioning.

'We've checked,' he said. 'Can you hear?'

'Yes.'

'Cyn's been busy, haven't you?'

'Whore,' breathed Keegan. 'Stinking, lying whore.'

63

'Don't!' said Sean, and the woman lowered her hand. 'You're pig in the middle, aren't you, Keegan? But you've been a dirty spy and we can't have that, no we can't. It doesn't make any difference to us, Keegan, you hear? You were hired by one of the Brits' intelligence agencies.'

'Christ!'

Keegan's mind was in a turmoil. He hadn't been set up by ordinary mobsters. Not criminals. Agents. Spies. Special Investigation Branch. The kind of informers that the Irish went berserk about. He, Keegan, had been set up by British Intelligence. Graves ran a spy bureau. It was like some crazy television sequence, but with a background of pain and blood instead of music.

'Start again, Keegan. What did they want you to do?'

'Mister, I just don't know anything about it.'

'You have to,' said Sean. 'You were brought in to drive the lorry.'

'I thought they were ordinary villains!'

'Stinking set of Judases!'

Keegan tried to make sense of it.

'Graves set me up,' he said.

'That's right,' encouraged Sean. 'We know, we had the word from someone who knows what goes on.'

'Graves had your daughter taken away,' the woman said quietly.

Keegan remembered the terribly mutilated doll. It would still be in the cab of the artic.

'Liar.' She had to be lying.

'They weren't very careful.'

'*No*!' Keegan's entire body was one huge spasmodic effort to stop her talking.

'She was hurt. She's had a brain haemorrhage. She's in hospital, Keegan.'

Sean watched him. The woman wasn't enjoying it. Anyone seeing Keegan's pain could only pity him. One of the ropes gave at his feet. Keegan felt it and kicked out. He hit empty air. Sean's gun was in his hand, a trick of legerdemain.

Then Keegan could voice and bellow his terrible fears. His voice boomed hollowly around the abandoned warehouse, echoing from the glass of the office, from the high ceiling and the grey walls, an animal shout of utter despair. There was nothing to be gained from him. He was out of his mind.

Sean clubbed him once, expertly.

TUESDAY

Sometime in the morning there was movement, noise, a rushing of feet and loud angry shouts. Keegan heard it vaguely. Concussion kept him from understanding, though he felt his ropes tighten.

'Jasus!' Sean bellowed, when one of the two burly dockers reported. 'Jasus, they've done for the whole of the Ardoyne Brigade – and the Falls Road Commissariat. The New Lodge stores too! We've men slaughtered!' Through the night, more information arrived at the Liverpool headquarters of the Provisional I.R.A.

During the quiet hours between twelve and one, men of the British Security forces moved throughout the torn province of Northern Ireland. Saracens slid into position. Small groups of Paras surrounded more than twenty locations. The radio-detection vans stayed at a distance. There were some surprises, for not all the locations were the traditional working-class houses or lonely barns or convent grounds. For instance, one signal came from the house of a wealthy and well-respected philanthropist, known for his abhorrence of violence. Another strong signal came from a Charity's headquarters. There was considerable quiet jubilation amongst the troops. They waited until one.

There was some opposition, sleepy men with guns blazing wildly. The troops were much better street fighters. Men died. They took only a handful of what they called terrorists, but the haul of arms was immense. Sean realized the extent of the damage during the course of Tuesday morning. He shook with emotion at each fresh piece of news.

'Jasus, we've been betrayed!'

He rushed off yelling his fury.

For Keegan, there was a long spell of fitful quietness. Towards midday, one of the minders remembered him.

'Do we feed this English bastard?' he said to his mate.

'It's a waste of time. He's due for the chop today.'

There was a reprieve. There had been more news from Belfast. In an Army operation as big as that of the night, there had to be a leak. It came from a woman telephonist manning a country exchange. She intercepted a message from a detector van which had broken down. She contacted her Brigade Commander, who was frantic over the seizure of arms. This was the first clue to come his way.

A man with some knowledge of electronics, he began to consider why a detector van should be at work in a remote country area near the Border. He checked. Several such vans had been sighted. It took only a few hours to root out the whole story. Northern Ireland had few secrets, and those soon became public property.

The first indication that the recent shipment of rocket-launchers was the key came when the pattern of Army raids was analysed by the more experienced I.R.A. commanders. All the arms caches raided had recently received the launchers.

They investigated. There had been the grossest kind of deception, a master-coup. The Brits had beaten them through the vilest treachery. It all led back to the shipment of rocket-launchers. There was only one conclusion possible. The driver of the lorry which had brought the rocket-launchers was a British agent.

What rocket-launchers remained were examined. They had been hidden deep underground. They were soon rendered safe.

The fury of the Provisionals was tempered by caution. Sean's instructions first drove him to outraged refusal, and then to puzzled acquiescence.

'I say we should shoot the fuckin' traitor and have done with it,' he blared down the telephone to his superior in Belfast. 'One less of they—'

'Sean Cassidy, you will do exactly as you are told,' said a schoolmasterish voice, which in fact came from a school-master. 'You will alert every cell in the London area and proceed according to the instructions I have given you.' In a more kindly way, the schoolmaster went on. 'Sometimes,

Sean, it's necessary to forgo the immediate punishment in order that the larger aims are fulfilled. One Ireland, Sean!'

'One Ireland,' said Sean, choking with emotion.

'It will come,' said the thin Belfast voice. 'Never fear, Sean. Now make it look good.'

'Yes sir,' Sean said, loud and martial.

Sean Cassidy made his way through the dingy Liverpool back-streets to the abandoned warehouse. He bitterly regretted what he was about to do. Nevertheless, he followed instructions to the letter.

Keegan heard footsteps and waited for death. He had tried again to stretch the biting rope. There was no strength left in him. Simply, his muscles refused to respond when he exerted pressure on the bonds. Nerves jumped and twitched. Nausea gripped him as he smelled his own waste. Self-disgust almost made him wish for the promised bullets.

He watched Sean approaching with the two lumpy-faced dockers. Memories clamoured around the inside of his head. He recalled a whimpering of sobbed pleasure and knew that Sean had coupled with the Englishwoman whilst he lay in a pain-soaked coma. Their sex, his suffering. Both of them aware that he might hear. Keegan felt helpless against the calculated perversity. And, after that, they had tried to make him believe that Ruthie was hurt. How could they invent such vileness? Ruthie's laughter echoed from some recess of memory. He quietened it by thinking of the pain in his shoulders and neck and guts. He didn't want Ruthie's memory present at his death.

'You're going to walk,' Sean said. He slashed and the ropes parted.

Keegan wanted to protest. He had wondered before why condemned prisoners walked to their execution, why they didn't scream and howl and kick. He knew now. They accepted the inevitable, even welcomed it. They were conditioned into acceptance. He tried to move his legs.

Through cracked lips he groaned his agony.

The two big dockers yanked him upright. He was propelled, legs dangling, to the big doors at the back of the warehouse.

Keegan would not accept it.

'I'm no part of it!' he yelled, hardly recognizing his own voice. 'Christ, man, who'll look after my girl!'

One of the burly dockers appeared to respond, but the other had a greasy sack ready. Instantly Keegan was in darkness with his terror. He yelled again, and the harsh sacking writhed into his mouth, a forewarning of the grave. Keegan struggled as they manhandled him into the van. He didn't see the exchange of silent questions and answers.

The van coughed into life and rattled along uneven surfaces. Then it joined a mainstream of traffic. Time passed again, time edging Keegan's life away. There was no chink of daylight, only blackness and helpless dread. Once, Sean spoke:

'This is an official execution, so it's to be done in the proper way. Liam, you do it. Two in the head. Make sure!'

'That I will,' came the easy brogue.

Keegan heard the gentle sliding of the bolt-action. He writhed against the bonds.

A little later Sean said: 'He can walk to the quarry.'

Keegan could imagine it, a worked-out sand or slate quarry a few miles out of Liverpool. There were dozens of them. He might lie a month before he was found. He tried to move his legs, but they were too numb. The bonds were gone, though, and life was returning.

He tried to judge the position of the three men. Two in the front, Sean driving and Liam watching, gun in hand. The other in the passenger seat. But three of them! Sean spoke again, directly to him:

'Keegan, there's nothing personal in this for any of us. You've been condemned to death by a properly constituted' – he stumbled over this, a lesson badly learned – 'Court of the Provisional Irish Republican Army. You're a dirty – you're an informer and a British agent discovered in an act of espionage. We're not murderers, we're soldiers. And you're being executed according to the articles of war.'

'Youse shouldn't have joined up,' said the other of the dockers. There was laughter in his voice.

Another that enjoyed killing. And yet did he look like a killer?

Sean looked at Liam. Liam nodded.

'Christ Jasus, there's a police barrier!' he yelled. 'Stop, Sean, stop!'

The van jerked. Keegan fell forward, his right elbow rammed a bulkhead. There was noise and confusion.

'Back the fuckin' thing!' bawled Liam.

The gears whined. Keegan felt the van shake and shudder as it reversed.

'Round the corner and away!' shouted Liam.

Then there was a ferocious clang.

'You've done us, Sean!' bawled the other docker.

The engine clattered as Sean tried to switch on the ignition.

'Get it away!' Keegan heard.

'I can't – the drive's gone!'

'Away lads – scatter!'

'Out!' yelled Sean.

'What about the fuckin' spy!' Liam shouted.

'They'll hear the shots – no!' Sean yelled.

Keegan hauled himself to his knees. His head swam with the effort. Only slowly did he realize he was alone. He could feel the wind blowing on to his hands. The door of the van was open. He brought his hands to his face. He could just hook one finger on to the stuff of the hood. It came off easily. Sunlight streamed into the back of the van, dazzling Keegan. Keegan heard himself sobbing. His hands shook like an old man's. He pushed up and stumbled headlong. Blood trickled from his knuckles. There was the sharp staccato bark of a small motor-cycle nearby. Keegan frantically pushed against the pain in his knuckles. He had to get away.

Deep, sullen tremors shook his legs. He pushed and crawled to the open doors. He saw he was in a suburban street, red-brick terraced houses half-demolished. The van was slewed at an odd angle. Still dazed by pain, the light lancing into his eyes, only half-conscious of his surroundings, he jack-knifed until his legs trailed over the back of the van.

When his feet touched the ground, feeling returned. He saw a fat youngish slattern pushing a pram. Two children straddled a younger one. Another child walked alongside, in the gutter. The woman looked at him. There was no curiosity in her gaze.

A cat brushed against his ankles. Keegan stumbled towards one of the houses. Then he stopped. The Irishmen might be hiding there. He turned back to the van. The cat mewed softly. Keegan looked down at his bonds and saw raw flesh at his wrists. He wondered what his face might do to people who saw him.

Police, the murderous bastards had said. Keegan grated a harsh laugh. So, for once, the law had helped him. It had saved his life. He thought, fleetingly, of making for the police barrier. It was a panic reaction, though. Keegan thought: What I've got to do is my affair. They'd not believe a word. It would be: Now, let's get this straight, Keegan, you say you've been kidnapped and British Intelligence is involved, eh, Keegan? Do you want us to believe that, really Keegan, what kind of story is that? We're not all big feet and helmets, Keegan, let's have the truth! 'No sardonic scuffers, not for me,' Keegan said aloud, not realizing he was talking to himself.

He stumbled away, holding his cruelly-torn wrists against his midriff. He ran then. Away from the menace of the soot-streaked houses, away from where the police were checking, away through an overgrown garden with two apple trees and to a derelict shed where he could hide and rest and find a slice of glass or a rusted spade to free his hands. Keegan didn't need time for reflection. He had to believe what his instincts told him about the Irishmen. They were long gone from the immediate vicinity. The Provos knew the tenacity of the scuffers.

Luck was with him from the start. There was a shattered pane of glass. Keegan held it between his shaking knees, carefully slicing through the blood-hardened rope. It took an hour.

He waited till dark before he moved. If his face looked like his wrists, he would be taken for a dazed crash victim and reported. Shattering pain lanced through Keegan's jaw. The broken tooth. It should be extracted. Time enough when the other thing was done. Keegan didn't think of a future. First, check that Ruthie was all right. She had to be. The Irish lied as easily as they breathed. Keegan trampled the bitter speculation.

When the one thing you loved was threatened, it became so much easier. There was a cold, eager joy in the simplicity of vengeance.

This time the message went through Dublin, for security had been tightened to an almost paranoiac level.

'Code Green-Three,' said Sean from the Manchester phone-booth.

'Acknowledged,' said the educated voice, and Sean thought of the easy life they led in the South, no risks, no night-raids, no blood on their smooth white hands.

'Please make your report, Green-Three.'

'Tell Belfast he's hooked.'

'And that's all, is it?'

'That's all you have to know.'

The speaker sighed. There was a longing for excitement in that sigh. 'Acknowledged. Good hunting.'

Sean put the phone down without speaking again. He rang a Liverpool number next.

'Well?' he said.

'He's still in the shed. He'll not move till nightfall.'

'Remember what you were told.'

'I'll remember. Observe only.'

'And don't follow!'

'I have it, Sean.'

'And no names over the phone!' yelled Sean, slamming the receiver down. English-Irish, Irish-English, cocky Southerners! He longed to be back in the Falls Road again. It was almost a year since his last kill.

TUESDAY NIGHT

Without money or identification of any kind, it is still possible to travel in Britain in relative comfort and at speed. Keegan had cleaned himself as best he could in the long, cool, damp grass. The dried blood was gone. His denim jacket turned inside out and dusted with lime to hide the worst of the stains. He could keep his wrists covered, and he could disguise the limp. He knew he stank.

He moved at dusk, when the streets were neither quiet nor busy. From the houses which hadn't yet fallen derelict, came men and women seeking refreshment: pub, chip shop, bingo parlour. Keegan limped along with them, retching with hunger and pain, but moving silently and steadily towards the sound of traffic.

The district was new to him, but the layout was no different from that of any large old suburb. He found the direction of the main road by picking out the glow of the sodium lights. A small group of youths watched him carefully as he passed the entrance to a community centre. He sensed their intoxication, not with alcohol but with the thought of beating up a vulnerable stranger, an enemy, an intruder.

He hurried past, eyes down. There were six of them, two large and booted. It was no time to get involved in a teenage brawl. One of them flicked a lighted cigarette at his feet. Keegan's mouth jetted with longing. A cigarette. A beer. Hot food. Deliberately he ground his broken tooth against a good one. The pain shocked him into bitter resolve. The youths watched him limp into the glare of the main road.

Keegan kept walking.

It was no use trying to hitch-hike in a strange town. There were too many knowing sods who might pass on the word that a battered and obviously drunken character was on the road: what was more, a big-shouldered brute with a furtive, stumbling, limping gait. At night, too, obviously trying to get away from some villainy.

Keegan limped past a row of shops. A barbecued chicken take-away was doing a brisk trade. Keegan felt through his pockets for the tenth time. Nothing. Kevin and the dockers had searched again, after Sean had taken all his papers and money. He hadn't eaten in two days. For much of the time he had been vomiting, and then choking on blood.

A car started up behind Keegan. A girl laughed and threw a wrapped something out of the window. Keegan watched it fall. The remains of a quick snack. He looked around. A black and white dog was interested. Keegan bent down. The dog whined at his feet. Keegan walked on, hands trembling. He snarled at the dog. It left, tail wagging, a look of great surprise on its face.

There was a surprising amount of meat on the bones. She must have fed before this, or perhaps she couldn't bring herself to suck the tendrils of dark meat from the legs. Keegan could. It hurt, cramped stomach muscles complained, but the food stayed down. A beer-shop invited him. He hurried away. No loitering, or the beat-man would be informed. They had their little two-way radios. Keegan moved on, faster.

He had to walk two miles before he oriented himself, and another two miles to find a junction which gave a through route to Yorkshire. After that, it was a matter of finding the right lorry. Some haulage firms wouldn't allow lifts; and it was no use signalling to someone who had a co-driver or a woman in the cab.

Keegan felt exposed under the high lamps. There was no help for it. Three times, police cruisers came near, but he could stand back in the shadow of a huge road sign. Either they did not see him or they chose to ignore him. And all the time, Ruthie was in danger. But no one could know she was at her Aunt Edie's. No one. How could they know? It was a vicious lie. The mutilated doll? You could buy a doll like Miss May anywhere.

Keegan made himself believe it.

When the lorry came, it was perfect: a driver not much older than Keegan, one who recognized that he was probably a fellow-driver. His Yorkshire taciturnity was welcome. He stopped at a motorway cafe and paid for the tea without a hint of condescension. He didn't mention Keegan's battered face and torn clothes. When they parted – he drove a dozen miles out of his way to save Keegan's time – there was only a monosyllabic exchange: 'Sure you're all right?' 'Thanks. See you.' 'See you.'

Keegan didn't go home. The Irishmen knew where he lived. And it was no use trying to get to Ruthie in his present state. Nor the other one: *Viney*. He needed to recuperate. There was a woman he could trust.

Like a wounded animal, he needed a few hours of rest, a

73

chance to lick his wounds. He could feel the change coming himself: tall, wide-shouldered and normally erect, he had unconsciously adopted a hunched appearance. He moved slower than usual, the weight of his heavy body further forward, almost the lope of an animal. It was two in the morning when he turned into a council estate three miles out of Sheffield.

The bright chimes seemed to fill the quiet cul-de-sac. The house was without movement. Keegan looked back. No beat-coppers in these parts. They used cars, kept their fat arses warm. Keegan checked his mounting hatred. He mustn't show it.

He rang again and tapped on the window to his left. A cat yowled nearby. Keegan wanted to slump down on the door-step. It wasn't a cold night. If he could rest up, just for a few hours. Then a hot bath. Someone to push the aching joints around, ease the torn muscles as little Jim Ashton, the trainer, used to. After a hard game he would be available to push and pull at ankles wrenched, knees ricked, shoulders jolted in bone-grating challenges. Keegan could feel the powerful, bony fingers on his neck where the chair-leg had gashed him, little Jim's clever hands pushing pain away. He thought: Thank Christ it isn't worse. He might have broken my bloody neck.

The pain flared afresh.

'Don't!' bawled Keegan, waking. He fell into the house, taking the woman with him.

'Terry! Look at you, oh look at your face!'

Keegan disentangled himself, groaning with fatigue and pain.

'Jen, don't yell!'

'But what have you done—'

Keegan grabbed her and held her mouth against his chest. Jennifer Roberts couldn't resist the direct appeal. Her muscles relaxed and Keegan felt her surge of passion. Her nipples pinked out as big as cherries. Amazingly, he felt the fire begin in his loins. She sensed his urgency and pulled away at once.

'Terry, keep quiet – the kids aren't well! Joan's got her bronchitis back, and Johnny keeps wandering when she coughs. Come on – into the kitchen! And for God's sake, Terry, what happened?'

Keegan stumbled after her. Now that he was safe, he could begin to think of the plans he had held back during the desperate hours of flight. First, though, Jen had to be reassured.

'I'm all right, Jen – just a bit of a punch-up. Nothing, love! You know me. I'd like some tea, though. And a wash. Bacon sandwich?'

She was staring at his neck.

'God, love, you're in a mess – you're hurt bad!'

Keegan felt his neck. The cut was deeper than he had realized. 'It's just a nick.' His broken tooth jarred and he winced. It should come out soon. 'Got some disinfectant? Cotton-wool?'

'You need a doctor! Go to the out-patients', Terry!'

Keegan took her hands. 'No police, no doctors.' She turned away, face suddenly empty of expression. Jen Roberts knew the score. She had worked the clubs too, before she married the dapper little clerk from London; she knew a little of Viney. Enough not to ask questions. When her little clerk stole the housekeeping and rent money and left her for the seventh or eighth time, she had asked Viney to pass on the word that he wouldn't be welcome home again. That was when Keegan met her, after a lapse of six years. By that time, she had Joan and Johnny. Keegan visited her occasionally. Both saw other partners, neither discussed them. It was an arrangement that suited them, for they needed the comfort of a shared bed from time to time.

'Jen, I'll be away before the kids wake.'

'What are you mixed up in?'

'Leave it. I'll be away before the kids stir.'

'You can't go like this!'

'Keep out of it, Jen. Please?'

'Is it Viney?'

Keegan thought: If it is, I'll have to kill him. If he's done the unthinkable and somehow put the finger on Ruthie he's dead. Another thought struck him: When Viney heard the set-up had failed, he'd come looking.

75

'Jen, no one saw me coming. I'm sure of it. Now, say nothing! I've not been here, understand?'

The broad pink face crumpled. She was scared. Her fear ran through her ample body. Keegan saw the drooping line of her generous breasts and remembered her from nearly ten years back, a figure like Marilyn's. He put an arm around her again.

'I promise, nothing will happen. I just want a shirt and a pair of trousers. And that old yellow sweater of mine. And a bath, Jen. I'm done.'

She ran the bath and shrieked at the marks and gashes. But she kneaded his muscles, plastered the big gash, bandaged his wrists and finger, disinfected the many grazes. Keegan lay back and fell asleep.

Then Jen was back, gently shaking him, her eyes awash with pity.

She had the food ready. Keegan wolfed it, ignoring the sharper bursts of pain from his broken tooth. As he drank hot, strong tea, stiff with sugar, he felt alive again.

'Bed,' he mumbled when he had finished. Jen led the way. 'Get me up at seven.'

Yet he could not sleep immediately, despite the thick soft mattress and the swathing duvet. Jen's body pressed warmly against him. Her great billowing breasts rode against his back. Keegan turned, and strength slid into his loins. Jen sobbed and reached, and he let her soft, agreeable thighs cradle his aching body, and afterwards sleep came down like the end of time.

WEDNESDAY

She woke him carefully.

'Terry, I love you, but you will keep me out of it won't you – I've the kids and I can't lose my job at the Stores.' She was weeping again. Keegan tried to harden himself against her tears. He couldn't. She was, like him, too ready to trust, a victim, not one of the stone-faced. 'I've only got this in the house,' she wept, pushing the crumpled notes into his hand.

Keegan took one pound note.

76

'I promise nothing's going to hurt you or the kids,' he said thickly. 'Jen, I won't let it.'

She rushed silently from the bedroom in a billow of cheap nylon lace, her heavy body still aromatic of love and her heavy cheap scent. Keegan left by the back door. Behind him, he heard a child's racking cough. It hit him like a knife-thrust.

Ruthie.

Keegan drew on his reserves of stamina. There was time enough for sleep when the thing was over. Head down, he loped towards a bus stop. Apart from the limp and the plasters, he would pass for a morning workman. The hunched posture concealed the sad fury in his eyes.

Keegan caught himself muttering aloud: 'Viney, it has to be. He's been trying to set me up since I took Tina.' Then it came to him again that the prison sentence had been Viney's work. The charge wouldn't have stuck if the witnesses had been the usual kind of customer. They had been so clear about what happened when they were giving evidence; they hadn't been scared of Viney as they should. Keegan's face looked gaunt as he surveyed the ruins of his life.

Viney.

Viney hated so long, so well.

Nobody should hate like that. Keegan loped through the thin drizzle. He was trying to recall a memory. It came as he remembered the look on the face of a former Second Division player he had met during his own playing days. That man had been a good hater. He was a Scot – name? wondered Keegan, name? Short, something like Hague or Hagan. A small, compact frame, grizzled hair. The story was simple. Hagan, if that was his name, had been badly fouled by one of the old-time backs. Smashed down, viciously, deliberately, and put out of the game for the rest of the season. A hard man, known and feared in his day. Hagan had waited sixteen years for his revenge. By a sudden trick of memory Keegan had total recall of the conversation: 'Ah saw him in this pub, doon London, aw mon, he was fou with the drink – big as ever, but fat and his legs gone. Aye. I went after him and cotched him doon a ginnel. He didn't know what hit him! Ah tellt him, but he didn't know it was Jock Hagan.'

Keegan recalled the intense satisfaction of the little Scot. 'Ah smashed his ribs for him, both sides.'

Viney. Graves. The loud-mouthed Irishmen and their murderous talk. They were linked in a chain of events that centred on him. And poor, stick-thin Ruthie. Keegan shuddered. Rage tautened the long muscles of his neck and shoulders. He could feel the itching, creeping infection of rage at the tips of his fingers, and then in the muscles below his torn wrists and through them to the ropy strength of biceps and back to his hunched shoulders. His entire body throbbed with rage. He nursed his rage on the slow bus journey to Auntie Edie's in company with the reluctant early workers.

He was careful. He moved in and out of corridors, through dark passages, pausing every so often to check. There was no one behind him; no one knew about Jen. No one could have followed without revealing themselves. The flats were a nineteen-fifties mistake, a great sooty tower stinking of poverty, littered with broken glass, and greasy paper. Keegan didn't try the lifts. They wouldn't be working. He was limping badly by the time he reached the eighth floor. The curtains weren't drawn.

Keegan peered in. A porcelain smile looked back, a treasure from a junk shop or jumble sale, probably stolen. The little statuette lifted a flared dress in one long-fingered hand. The left arm was broken. Keegan remembered the doll. Keegan shook, dread seizing him once more. *Ruthie was all right.* He thumped softly on the window. Only the police knocked sharply at the door at this time of the day.

It took ten minutes to rouse her. When she came, she didn't know him. She peered through the glass, searching a booze-soaked brain and soon giving up.

'Sod off!' she croaked. 'I don't want anything.'

'It's me, Terry! Open up – open up, Edie. Open the bloody door,' he snarled, low and savage.

She understood the tone.

'Who is it?'

'Terry – I want Ruthie!'

'She's gone.' Keegan heard, and he drew his fist back to drive it into the wizened, toothless face of his mother's elder

78

sister. The door creaked as she fumbled at the lock. Keegan pushed. He looked at the old lined grey skin. She wasn't sixty yet, but she had the look of the dead, her face bloomed with decay.

'I just want Ruthie,' he said quietly. 'I'll take her home now.' Aunt Edie wouldn't recover from the night's stupor till late afternoon. Keegan realized that, after all, the thin woman had not lied. Ruthie wasn't there. She'd have come running by now.

'Oh, they took Ruthie!'

The surging panic was back.

'Who?' grated Keegan.

'The Welfare, 'course. Like last time!'

When he had been in gaol, the old cow had neglected Ruthie, then the Welfare people had stepped in. It had taken months after his release to convince them he was the right person to care for her. Keegan held on to his sanity by a huge effort.

'Did they say they were Welfare?'

It was too much. Pin-point pupils tried to focus. Auntie Edie's chin nodded down. She would fall into her usual coma soon. The place stank abominably. Keegan wondered how he could live with himself.

Carefully, Keegan angled the woman into a chair. He propped her head in his hands.

'Wake up.'

She stirred. Her eyes opened.

'It's Terry!'

'Yes. Ruthie. You were telling me they took Ruthie.'

'They did!'

'What did they look like?'

'Fellers!' Edie yelled. 'Just fellers.' Then she remembered. 'One looked like Charlie Chan, except he hadn't got the moustache.'

Keegan trembled. *Nider*. Asiatic features, like those of the detective she remembered from the thirties films. Nider's flat face. Nider's huge hands on Ruthie. But how did they know she was here? How!

He could have snapped her neck. Instead, he made his voice low and soothing:

79

'What happened then?'

'I don't know, Terry! They didn't tell me. They said it would be all right. No harm done.'

'Where is she?'

'I don't know!'

Then she remembered. 'One of the gentlemen said she'd have to go to the hospital.'

It was true.

Keegan forced the knowledge on himself.

'Which hospital?'

The old woman closed her eyes and sagged back.

Keegan turned away. There weren't so many hospitals. Only one, when it came down to it, a large teaching hospital famous for its treatment of children. Keegan left and shut the door gently.

Inquiries were handled by a staff of almoners. Keegan had to wait whilst an old man argued about money and then again when the phone rang. He wondered why the phone should take precedence. It always seemed to. He tried to take an interest in the people he saw: in a surly child of seven or eight who didn't want to sit quietly; in a gaunt woman with a baby, very tired; in the conversation of two women clerks, chirpy at half-past eight, loving life. Anything to block off thought and memory.

'Yes?' said the smiling, middle-aged woman.

'My little girl's been hurt. I was away on a trip.' He rushed the words. 'How is she?'

'Your name, please?'

'Keegan.'

'And what is your little girl called, Mr Keegan?'

She had seen the red-edged welts on his face. Keegan kept his voice calm.

'Ruthie. Ruth.'

'And your address?'

He told her. 'But she was at the flats. Staying with her auntie when she was hurt.'

The woman looked at cards. 'Ruth Keegan?'

She was there.

'Yes.'

'And you are the father?'

'Yes.' Keegan saw the hesitation. 'I was driving. From Belgium. She hasn't got a mother. Can I see her?'

'She's in the Intensive Care Unit, Mr Keegan. I think the surgeon who operated will let you look. Will you take a seat whilst I ring through?'

The words numbed him. Time passed, and he was handed to a cadet nurse, who in turn took him through wide corridors, wide archways, wide doorways, until they came to the Unit. A sharp-faced young sister took over. Sit. Wait. Another ten minutes, and an exchange of glances between the sister and a young Indian doctor. Keegan forced himself to stillness. The surgeon came, dark-suited and prosperous, with fat white hands.

Keegan listened.

'It's not a bad fracture, Mr Keegan, I don't want you to think that. What makes little Ruth's case so severe is the length of time it took to get her to hospital. You see, in a case of this kind—' Keegan glared at him so savagely that he stopped. 'Mr Keegan?'

'It's been a shock,' said the sister. 'He's only just learned about his daughter, Mr Brough. Mr Keegan, are you all right?'

'How bad is she?' Keegan said. 'Will she live?'

'I think so, Mr Keegan,' said Mr Brough carefully. 'She has every chance, but it's early to be sure. I think I've told you all I wish to at this stage. Except that I'm sorry. You'll wish to see her, of course. This way, Mr Keegan.'

Keegan followed. 'I left her with that drunken old cow. I hadn't got anyone else.'

'Nobody's blaming you,' said the sister. 'Ruth wouldn't. Please be very quiet.'

Keegan saw muted light, a tiny, pinched face, sunken eyes, a mass of gauze, the thin frame hardly disturbing the even line of the cover. He thought: Dear Christ, I've raised Ruthie in a stinking hole like Dunkerly Street. I left her with an old drunk like Edie. So she would be safe. And they went straight to her.

'Come away now,' said the sister.

'You can come anytime,' said Mr Brough. 'Ring anytime, day or night. We're doing all we can. Now you look all in. Could you get him a cup of tea, Nurse?' he said to the cadet. 'I think Ruth has a good chance,' he told Keegan.

Keegan didn't hear.

'How did they know she was at Edie's?' he said.

'Come away,' said the sister.

Keegan allowed himself to be led.

'Go to your own doctor, Mr Keegan,' said Mr Brough. 'You've not been in an accident yourself, have you?'

'Someone told them,' said Keegan. 'Who?' He stared at the Sister, at Mr Brough, at the Indian's round, dark face. 'It couldn't have been Viney, could it. He wouldn't know about Ruthie's aunt.'

'Go home,' said the Indian doctor.

The Sister said:

'By the way, there are some questions—'

Keegan didn't hear. He moved away.

'I know who it was,' he said, a sudden image of the past rearing before him. 'It was her. She knew.' He was living in another world by now. 'I'll kill her.'

He heard Mr Brough's educated voice full of concern. *Shock. Treatment.* And then he was moving faster, the pain of the leg nothing at all now. He was a spear launched, a living projectile that knew its target.

She lived in a pleasant suburb of Sheffield, a short bus-ride from the hospital, then a walk of ten minutes. Keegan tried to recall her features. He couldn't. Her legs yes, her face no. Slender, well-muscled legs, a neat set of hips, not much in the way of tits, but moving like a hungry cat, always pacing about the club, watching and waiting.

In a fit of sentiment she wanted pregnancy and marriage. And got it.

Now she was married again. Keegan hadn't seen her since he was in gaol, then only to sign papers to hand over the little money he had. For Ruth. For Ruth's sake, not hers. Keegan remembered the address because he had chanted it through one bad night when he wanted to hurt Tina. When he had done his time, it hadn't mattered, for there was the prospect of Ruthie's return to him.

'Nine Acacia Avenue,' Keegan murmured, reaching the tree-lined street in a tree-dark suburb. Green was everywhere. The garden blazed with flowers. A Mini stood in the drive. She answered the door, and he knew her at once.

'Terry!' Then she tried to get the door shut, for his face was like a slab of torn rock. 'No!'

He pushed her inside. His hands went to her neck, thin and wiry still, all the young fat melted away in the onset of middle age. Her breath stank.

'You rotten bitch!' Keegan whispered. 'Oh, you dirty rotten bitch!'

He had forgotten why he was there. All the pent-up hatred surged. Her eyes were wide, white all around them. A creaking sigh came from thin, painted lips. Keegan saw the bright red of her lips and the dull red of her face. He dropped her.

'—get the dog!' she was trying to croak. 'I'll get the dog!'

There would be no dog. Tina had always hated dogs, but she'd know what to say, quick lies – her husband was in the garden, the dog in the kitchen. Scare off the intruder, get time to run for help. Keegan sighed and remembered why he had come. She had betrayed her child. Keegan bent and picked her up.

He showed his fist. Her eyes went down to the lacerated knuckles.

'Oh don't, Terry, don't, you rotten bleeder, *don't*!' She was squealing again, too loud. Keegan hit her, not hard, in the midriff. She doubled. Before she fell, he caught her. There was no flesh on her. He almost panicked, for a recollection of an old tenderness made him fear he had damaged her.

'Don't scream again,' he said quietly. He let her fall. She was retching. His stomach muscles twitched in sympathy. 'I don't want to hurt you, Tina, I don't.'

'—bastard, oh, you bleeder – if Arthur was here, he'd kill you—' Then she retched again, bile trickling through the bright scarlet lips. Her face was white now, bloodless. Her fists beat the floor. 'I'll get the police!' She glared up at him. 'They'll not let you have her back.'

Keegan's foot was already moving. She had said the unspeakable. He stopped the kick just in time. It would have

83

killed her, for it was aimed at the point where the thin neck met the skull. He panicked again and thought: Christ, if I kill her, what do I get? Nothing! – not Viney, not Graves, not Ruthie! Keegan, *hold back!*

He lifted her. 'Listen.' He slapped her once, twice. 'I don't *care*. Get that through your snake's head. *I don't care.* Ruthie's in hospital. Those goons who came here did it—'

'Ruthie! No, Terry, no!'

It wasn't the news of Ruthie's hurt that brought the denial. There was a bright, furtive calculation in her eyes. She knew the score in that second. Keegan saw it. He hit her again, slowly. Once, twice, across her mouth. Blood sprang out of the right side, brighter than the lipstick.

'If—' he said, spacing the words '—if you don't tell the truth, Arthur won't know you when he gets home.' He remembered now. Arthur was a grocer. The Mini would be Tina's. 'Listen.' Keegan held his hand ready. 'Who came for Ruthie?'

'No—'

Keegan's hand slashed her again.

'No one,' she screamed.

Keegan was weary. Tina lied as kids stole sweets. It had to be done. Viney could do this. Any of Viney's mob. Nider could both do it and enjoy it. The photographs and the fiendishly mutilated doll proved it.

'You were the only one who knew about Ruthie's Aunt Edie.' It was as sad and final as the words at a funeral.

'Terry, you've hurt me! Shit, I know you're mad, but believe me, believe me, no one—' Tina realized that she faced death. The insolent lies faded away. She breathed hard, pain filled her face. 'They came Friday night, Terry! Arthur was mad!' Her head snapped back, away from the blow she expected.

Keegan released her. She fell back against the wall, shuddering with relief, knowing he would not hit her again.

'Who?' The cruelly mutilated doll had been in the cab of the lorry on Saturday. 'You knew them?'

'You shouldn't hit a woman! Call yourself a man – no, Terry!'

'I haven't got time for this crap.'

84

'All right! One was Gus, I didn't know the other. He was young.'

Viney's goons.

'Tall, thin?

'Yes, Terry! But don't go to Viney, don't, Terry! Don't tell him I said anything, will you?'

Keegan saw the tortured, twisted, sly face and wondered how he could have loved her. And he had. It wasn't just a few white hot nights like so many in the club days. Then, she seemed to have a wild charm; she radiated happiness when he was about. Had it been all deceit, a drawn-out lie?

'Does your husband know about Viney?'

Alarm filled the thin face. 'Don't tell him! You wouldn't, Terry? He doesn't know anything!'

'Is that your Mini outside?'

She was ahead of him. 'Arthur wouldn't let me lend it – Terry, don't take it, it's mine!'

The surly voice, the greedy child's yell. The years rolled back and Keegan wondered how she had produced Ruthie.

'Keys.'

She read the message well. 'Mind the paint, won't you, Terry – be careful with it! You'll let me know when I can have it?'

'I'll do that.' He paused. 'Report it stolen tomorrow night. Not before.'

'Yes, Terry.' As an afterthought, she said, 'What's the matter with Ruth?'

'They'll tell you at the hospital.'

A shadow of remorse passed over the thin, pallid face. 'Was it an accident?'

Keegan was at the door. He thought of Nider's flat face. He couldn't answer.

Viney's house was impressive. Red-brick, with turrets and mullioned windows, and a porch almost as big as the house in Dunkerly Street. It was set in an acre of garden. Keegan drove through the wide-open iron gates with memories crowding him. Viney had bought the place ten years back. Once, there had been parties. Guests had to get drunk. Viney liked to see them swaying and stumbling about the grounds. He would tease his girls so they fought one another, then he would lead them, spitting and scratching, to the pool. He was the king, they had to clown for him. Tina had stripped one night, Keegan watching her in disbelief as Viney's cold eyes glittered in the lantern-light. It was the first Keegan had known of her sordid and contemptuous faithlessness.

Gravel spun under the wheels. The oak doors opened and two men ran from the house. Keegan knew at once: she had rung Viney.

One was Gus, the other the youth who liked to have a brick in his hand. Both were shouting but the Mini's revving drowned what noise they made. Brick-boy had a pick-axe handle, standard equipment at Viney's house, kept in an umbrella stand. He raised it and jeered.

Keegan could have spun the Mini over the lawns and retreated. Brick-boy thought he would and anticipated the move. Gus ran right, the boy left. Brick-boy had the pick-axe handle raised to smash in the windscreen, just as he had seen it done on the films. The Mini sprayed gravel as Keegan drove at him. He stayed his ground, incredulous.

Keegan saw the sudden realization of disaster on his long, bronzed face. His teeth were bad. The small car hit him solidly, folding him across the bonnet with a dull, wet-sounding thump. Keegan heard his screams. Then he was gone under the left wheel. Gus threw his pick-axe handle. Keegan watched it cart-wheel towards the windscreen. He turned the car and felt the jolt as Brick-boy's body went under the rear wheels. The wooden stave clanged against the roof and ricochetted away towards the house.

The spin of the car took him within ten yards of the door. Keegan slammed on the brakes. Even so the Mini mounted the porch. Glass showered as the side windows went. Then Keegan stumbled out. Gus ran to the twitching body.

'Shit, what have you done to Alan!' He turned to Keegan and looked for the pick-axe handle. It lay near the porch. Keegan saw the shock, outrage turn to doubt and fear. 'Keegan, you've killed the lad!'

Keegan bent for the thick wooden stave. 'Where's Viney?' he shouted hoarsely.

Gus knew when to call on reinforcements. 'Geordie!' he yelled, and Keegan remembered the thick-bodied yob who had known about alley-fighting. He heard the sound of a man coming fast, heavy footsteps partly muffled by thick carpet. He turned as the squat figure hurtled through the porch. The club swung in a wide arc. It was like hitting a brick-wall. The pick-axe handle bounced off the thick skull with a dull cracking sound.

'Oh Christ,' said Gus, quitting. Keegan motioned with the club. 'Viney.'

'Behind you,' Keegan heard. 'Don't!'

Keegan was already whirling. He saw the wide double mouth of the shotgun and, behind, Viney's plump face, with the cold eyes keen as ever, but the hands were slack and the body shaking. Keegan threw the pick-axe handle in a scything arc. Viney saw and jerked at the triggers, both of them.

Keegan dived as the double explosion boomed and echoed throughout the great, high hall. The air above him split. A huge sighing shout followed and then Keegan was jerking a surprisingly spindly leg for a man of Viney's bulk. Viney went down. Already off-balance, he was stunned by the noise and effects of the blast.

Keegan forced himself to his knees then to his feet in the old way when you *had* to be up before the goal-mouth scramble was over and the game fifty yards upfield. Gus yelled then, and Keegan staggered on his bad leg. Viney was bawling the outraged obscenities of fear. Keegan kicked down with his heel and felt the ligaments in his right leg burn with agony. Viney lay still after that.

Gus made some sense as the three of them choked breath back into their lungs.

'Look at the poor bastard!'

Keegan looked. Terrible choking sounds came from the Geordie. He was face down. Gus walked slowly and turned him over. He and Keegan saw the red gruel and white splinters. The blast had caught the left side of the man's face. It was clear he couldn't live. Viney whimpered as Keegan almost leisurely showed him the stained baton. For Keegan, the moments of violence had almost the quality of a dream.

The separate incidents were self-contained, linked only by the spasmodic yet strangely logical leaps which occur in nightmares. Brick-boy was floating away from the side of the red car. Gus coming in fast but with no enthusiasm at all. A pick-axe whirling with a deliberate speed. The bone-crushing lurch as the small wheels pounded the youth into the gravel. Then the Geordie, no fear in his face, a small scar livid over his left eye. Flame, dark smoke, the air shivering with force-waves. Viney, realizing that he was beaten, whimpering. The terrible face, no scar now, red ruin.

Keegan felt his hands trembling. Reaction. He had seen it on the football field. An arm badly broken could do it, or an ankle suddenly snapped. The others were in a worse state. Viney, up now on one elbow, was whimpering. Gus tried not to vomit over the twitching body of the Geordie. Keegan's mind worked slowly, or so it seemed to him.

One, maybe two dead. The Mini battered by the porch column. No use now, no use anyway, for Keegan had seen how the dragnet worked. The police would guarantee that a known car they really wanted would be picked up within the hour. England was a small country. Keegan shuddered once. Then he could act.

'Get up,' he told Viney.

There was no fight left. The man's eyes vowed revenge, but there was no courage left. Viney was thinking of the blood and the noise and his carefully guarded position as a respectable businessman. Keegan could see into the warped, brilliant mind as if a window had opened in his head.

'You're dead,' Viney whispered, but it was habit, this threat. He watched the baton carefully.

'My daughter may be dying. You did that.' Keegan saw the reaction; Viney knew. 'Tina told you. When she said I was on the way. Viney, you have to believe me; there's nothing else in the world but Ruthie. Nothing. I have to get to the swine who did it. Believe me,' said Keegan. 'Now get Gus to see to that,' he said pointing to the Geordie. One eye was open to the rain. 'And that.' He indicated the long, broken body of the youth. The twitching had stopped.

'Don't tell me what to—'

'Now!'

Keegan laid the heavy staff on the back of Viney's neck. 'You do exactly what I say, Viney, or I finish you here and now. You know why.' He read the man's mind. Keegan nodded. 'You know why. Tina told you about Ruthie.'

Viney looked down. He did not dare show defiance. Already he would be thinking about the fate of those who went to prison after hurting kids: English criminals had a blind spot for those who offered violence to children.

'Gus,' said Viney. The big, round-shouldered figure jerked. 'Get them out of sight – quick!'

Gus shambled forward, vomit dribbling down his sweater. His face was grey, but he was strong. He picked up the broken body of the youth and carried it without effort past the two heavy-breathing men.

'I want one thing from you,' said Keegan. 'An address.'

'I don't have to take this,' snarled Viney, suddenly revived.

'Oh, you do. You do. You set me up and I should be dead, but they took Ruthie!' Keegan heard his own voice too loud. Gus stumbled past for the corpse of the Geordie. 'The one good thing in my life! And you, you shit, you knew!'

The pick-axe handle seemed to go up of its own accord.

'No don't, Keegan! I didn't know about that – I wouldn't have done it, you great stupid bastard, no!'

Keegan knew how easy it would be to kill a man.

'You've been setting me up for years,' he said. 'That assault charge that came out Grievous Bodily Harm. Then the loan. You wanted me badly, didn't you?'

'Get off my back, Keegan! Haven't you done enough – for Christ's sake! I've got to get rid of Alan and Geordie, I can't do anything for you! I never touched the kid!'

'If I thought it was you, you'd be dead now. I want the bastards who did it.'

'It's a hard London mob, Keegan! I don't know them – I got the word they needed a driver, and you owed me! I didn't think it was a set—'

'No more lies. I'll break your arms, then your legs if you don't start talking.' Keegan was very calm, very alert. Viney watched the bulk of his shoulders and the swell of muscle in his right arm. Over the years, Keegan had remained hard.

He swallowed and thought of the Geordie's wrecked face, and the way the eager youth's bones seemed rubbery as Gus slung him up and over his shoulder.

'I don't know any names, Keegan,' Viney said. 'I got a message from a fixer. I don't even know his name, not properly, but he's the contact the big boys use when they want a job done up here. He's called Larry.'

'Larry.'

'Yes! And I don't argue. He fixed things for me, I do the same for his clients. We don't have to know their names, Keegan – it isn't done like a sodding garden party! He passes the word and fixes the price—'

'How much was I worth?'

Viney couldn't help grinning the familiar triumphant grin. 'I threw you in for nothing!'

'And Ruthie?'

Viney was another that knew he was near to death that morning. He saw the madness that had driven Tina to abrupt, icy rigidity.

'I didn't know they'd hurt the kid! I wouldn't have stood for it – shit, I wouldn't mess about with harming kids!'

'No.'

Viney knew what happened to child-beaters in gaol. The warders looked the other way. If Viney ever got a prison sentence, the word would soon get round. The sadists would work off their spleen in a righteous cause.

'Look,' said Viney, 'look, Terry, you've left me up shit creek with two deaders, two! My best boys! – what am I supposed to say? Do me in as well? Yes, shoot my arse off and make it a round score? I tell you, I don't know anything, and I can't do anything! I've got to find somewhere to put those two poor sods tonight, and if one word – one word! – gets out, I'm washed up! Two bastards to concrete up!'

'You've done it before.'

'Not two at once! Shit, I'm not the S.S.! I should get discount.'

Keegan interrupted:

'I want them, Viney! If I don't last another minute after I find them I've got to kill the bastards. Nothing else matters!'

'I don't even know who they are! All I saw was two blokes in a car! Who are they, anyway?'

There was a new note in Viney's voice. And Keegan believed him. He had known Viney for years, listened to his lies and watched his expert manipulation of the weak. There had been the other thing too: Viney had an insatiable curiosity about people; that was part of the secret of his success. Cunning and nerveless ruthlessness made up the rest. Now, he was curious. Who were they, he'd said.

'They'd eat you,' said Keegan.

'Whose mob is it? You've seen them?'

Two men waiting to be entombed in the foundations of one of the big new office blocks – two of his own men killed – and Viney was jostling for advantage, his small greedy eyes full of excitement. Why not tell him? With luck Viney might fall foul of them.

'S.I.B. It's a Provisional I.R.A. job. That's what you let me in for. If I see them or the Micks, shall I say Viney was asking?'

'Jesus, the S.I.B.? Government? Shit, Keegan, I don't want to know this!' Viney yelled. 'And the Provos! *Shit!*'

Viney was recovering fast. Alarm registered, then cunning. He was thinking about the shotgun. Even as his eyes flickered, Keegan said:

'Both barrels fired.'

Viney swallowed. 'Leave me out of it, will you? Haven't you caused me enough aggro? I didn't know it was police and sodding spies!'

'You must have a contact.' There had to be a phone number. 'Give.'

'And you'll leave me out of it?'

'What do you think?'

'It won't do you any good. Fixers keep well back from the action. I'll give you the number, and that's all.'

Keegan nodded. 'And money.'

'Money!'

'Four hundred and sixty-six pounds.'

'You owed me a bloody sight more than that!'

'You keep the lorry.' It wasn't likely that he would need it again. 'Get the money.'

Keegan watched the exasperation fade away as Viney worked out their relative positions. Finally, he shrugged. 'This way.'

Viney appeared not to notice as Keegan threw the shotgun away. He led the way to a large, book-lined room with an ornate walnut desk and water-colours of the Peak District. Keegan kept close, though he was fairly sure there would be no more guns. Viney was too careful to keep anything but a legitimate fire-arm in the house.

The money hadn't been touched. The elastic band was still in place. Keegan thought: If I'd been able to raise another few hundred Ruthie would be safe. He saw Viney watching him carefully. It struck Keegan that Viney looked scared.

'Get the number.'

Viney reached for the phone. He dialled quickly. Keegan listened. He could just hear the high-pitched whine. 'I can't get it!' Viney said.

'Maybe you misdialled.'

Viney flicked at the dial. The same numbers. He looked up, and Keegan saw that there was real fear in his face. 'That number's unobtainable.'

'Ring the operator.'

Viney held the ear-piece so they could both listen.

The voice was crisp and clear. 'I'm sorry, caller,' the girl said, 'the number has been withdrawn.'

'It wasn't on Friday!'

'I really can't provide any more information, sir. That number has now been withdrawn from service.'

'But didn't he leave another number?'

The girl stonewalled carefully. No further information would be forthcoming. Viney growled at her, slammed the receiver down, and looked up at Keegan. 'It was the right sodding number, Keegan – I've known it years! For Christ's sake, listen! I can see what's happened – as soon as the word got round that it was the long-raincoat lot, Larry would be up and out of it. They must know you're still around, Keegan! It's got back – you were supposed to be a patsy, you weren't supposed to be running around still! Larry's heard something. He's upped sticks and got out of it. He'll be out of the country on some sodding beach by now. That's where I'm going too. Keegan, listen to me! Stop!'

The pick-axe handle was smooth, heavy, tempting. Keegan had raised it high without realizing he had done so. He stared at Viney's terrified face. But it wasn't Viney who had so brutally manhandled Ruthie that her life was in danger. *Nider.* The blank-faced thug and the cold-smiling educated bastard. And behind them, the devil's mask of Graves. Keegan knew he would kill, as sure as he knew anything in the entire corrupt and sickening world.

'It won't do you any good to do me in, you silly bastard!' yelled Viney. 'Nor Ruthie. Listen – I've got to be around to get rid of my two boys. If I don't do it, Gus there will hang around like a bleeding zombie. He doesn't know what day it is! He hasn't got a price of doing anything to clear this mess up without me at his elbow! And if we don't get rid of the deaders, we'll have the law swarming around, and where are you? What can you do for Ruthie when you're in for life as accessory to murder? She won't see you until you're drawing your bloody pension! *Keegan!*'

Keegan could see sharply, even brilliantly. It was like looking through a range-finder in bright sunlight. Every detail of the room's furnishings glistened before him: red leather book-bindings, gilt titles, the two chandeliers tinkling and spinning with blue and red lights, the array of gold-plated pens, the ink-stand with its marble nude, Viney's coarse face with the little blue veins, the dull greys and blues of the bank-notes: and the carpet, all intricate shining yellows and greens and reds, Indian was it?

And Keegan knew something now, something that had been near when he had swum into frightful pain after the beating in the Liverpool warehouse The night of the long drive to London. There was a memory, if he could track it down. If he thought hard enough, if he flayed his brain, slit the core of memory and examined it strip by strip, then there *was* something.

What!

'All right, Terry?'

Keegan lowered the heavy club. 'You're nothing, Viney. You set me up, then a child. But you're right. I don't want the police after me, not yet. But get in my way again, turn me in, I'll be back.'

Viney shook his head. 'How can I convince you, Terry? All right, I set you up, but it's over! I'd no idea they'd go to your girl, none, Terry! And I won't be bothering you or anyone else ever again! Can't we just forget it? We're not going to kiss and make up, but we can keep out of one another's way? Eh?'

It made sense to leave Viney. 'You can tell Tina to pick up her car,' said Keegan.

He caught a bus into the centre of the town and went to a toyshop. The young assistant watched him with curiosity as he walked slowly along the line of cellophane-fronted boxes. At last, he made his choice. 'Don't wrap it,' he said.

At the hospital he saw the smiling-faced, middle-aged woman again. 'There's no change,' she told him. He explained about Miss May. 'It isn't exactly like her old doll, but there's not much difference. Will you see she gets it?'

The woman wanted to say more, but Keegan wouldn't let her. 'You'll be sure to see she gets it?'

'Yes, Mr Keegan. I'll make sure.'

The woman watched him thread his way through the groups of visitors and out-patients, a lonely and desolate figure; a man above medium height, square and solid, packed with hard muscle and, though limping slightly, marked off by that drawn face as *danger*. She shuddered and looked down at the doll.

She remembered her instructions then and ran after him.

'Oh, Mr Keegan!' she called. 'Just a minute please! There are some questions—' she began, then her voice was lost in the harsh jangling bell which indicated the arrival of an emergency case, and she had other things to do. For the time being, she forgot the man and his dangerous, grief-stricken face.

Keegan was passing through the main doors when the bell jangled nearby. He hadn't heard the woman. He stopped. A child walked into him. Its mother began to scold and then she looked, smiling, at Keegan. She hurried her brood on, appalled at what she saw. He didn't see her, nor her children in their bright raincoats. He was back in the recent past, trying to link the jangling, insistent noise of the ambulance with the journey to London.

94

He closed his eyes. A dark-skinned nurse stopped and asked him if he was ill. He didn't hear. She decided against repeating her question. Keegan ground the broken tooth until his jaw could not bear the pain. *Think!*

Think about the last few minutes, when you were coming out of the drugged sleep. Think about the bell . . . Think about waking up because you were cramped and so the right leg moved, and you hurt . . . There had been the roundabout. Very little traffic: the occasional dull roaring boom of a big vehicle, and a high-revving small car with loose tappets just after that. General traffic noise, nothing special, until the roadworks brought a smooth pressure on the brakes and three, no, four chicane-like bends. They were doing eighty or more on the straight runs. Then, deliberately, Bromley had taken precautions, confused him by making a number of nonsensical turns, first east through narrow lanes with high hedges that boomed back the motor's roar, then south. Keegan knew one of the minor roads. But Bromley was smart, well-trained, very careful, even though he thought Keegan asleep. He had completely disoriented Keegan by working his way round the gentle curves of a new housing development, so that afterwards, Keegan knew only that they must be moving somewhere on the outskirts of London and heading towards the centre. But there had been that bell. They should have used ear-plugs, thought Keegan. The noise of the ambulance had been unmistakable.

Ambulance: *accident.*

On most nights, the streets would have been quiet, but this was early Saturday morning after a warm sunny day, the beginning of a holiday weekend. The ambulance driver wanted a clear way through the traffic, so he had used his warning bell. And Bromley had cursed under his breath as he was forced into the side of the road to make way for the ambulance. Then the bell had stopped. Once Bromley drove on, they had taken only three minutes to reach their destination.

Keegan smiled. His luck had changed. But for the involuntary movement of his injured knee, he would have slept until he was in the secluded grounds. That was the intention. Bromley had taken precautions, but he had made

95

a mistake. One small error, caused perhaps by impatience or tiredness.

It wouldn't be difficult to find out where the accident had occurred.

Keegan looked back at the hospital. He saw the middle-aged woman and vaguely remembered that she had called him.

He cursed quietly at the recollection. *Questions.* Naturally. Ruthie hurt, so questions. Questions might mean an official inquiry. *Police.* A worse thought followed: Graves' people knew where Ruthie was. And so did the Irishman, Sean.

Graves felt his withered chest and counted the heart-beats. He wondered how long he would live. He hoped it would be for ever. Already there had been seventy-seven years of delicious perfidy and perversion. For decades he had sent alert, dedicated, brilliant men and women into extreme danger in a dozen countries, sometimes deliber-ately contriving their deaths when their detestation of his personal habits showed too well. He loved their hate, revel-led when they died. He was that rare creature, a human being who could not relate on personal terms to another human being. He lived through his schemings. His sex-life had always been unnatural, and it still puzzled him that he derived any pleasure at all from it.

Graves got up from the hot sauna bench and ran for the cold plunge. Ice-cold water slashed at his scrawny frame. He laughed aloud at his own wickedness. When he was dressing, he caught sight of himself in the gold-framed mirror.

'You pathetic old sweetheart,' he said crisply. 'I can't even feel sorry for you.'

Feeling better, he went to his office. Bromley was waiting.

'Well, Anthony?' he said. 'Don't say you're miserable too? How did your weekend go?'

'Well enough, sir, thank you. I've rather bad news though, I'm afraid.'

Graves was stimulated. 'Then begin, dear boy.'

'Keegan's loose.'

'Keegan – that coarse lorry-driver?'

'Rankin rang, very frightened. No, not here, sir, at my

96

private number,' Bromley added quickly. 'He doesn't know.'

'Rankin? The journalist? Tell me the rest.'

'He heard it accidentally, though he says the source is a good one. One of the Provisionals' Brigade Commanders. He was hanging around the Camden pub they use hoping to hear something about the execution of Keegan. When a member of the British Security forces, especially an under-cover operative, is killed, they have a celebration. It's not too open. More of a wake, but you know how the Irish behave at a wake, sir.'

'Only by hearsay.'

'There was something – some tension, but nothing that fitted the usual pattern. And there were some new faces, people Rankin hadn't seen. One of them was a Dubliner, out and out. Rankin thinks he's one of their top hit men, the sort they won't use in Northern Ireland in case he's com-promised. He was an educated fellow, but he looked a killer. The others were top brass from the North.'

'Do get to the point, Anthony.'

'Rankin heard a comment about the rockets. They're boiling with rage. You know, the Army had a very good haul. Most of their ready-use ammunition, their only heavy machine-gun, sixteen mortars, automatic weapons in scores. They're *very* annoyed. They want blood.'

'They had Keegan.'

'He escaped.'

Graves' strange black eyes clouded. There had been fouled-up operations before; but this was bad. An amateur breaking loose. He knew things, had seen things, could say things. He wouldn't know the rules.

'Get him picked up. Use a Group Four-One authorization – we can get it within ten minutes from Charles,' he said, naming a reactionary Under-Secretary. 'The police will have him within hours. He's to be wrapped up tight until we collect him.'

Bromley dialled as Graves spoke. Whilst he was waiting for the connection, he said: 'Keegan can't be such a fool as we thought.'

Graves smiled. It had been a most agreeable morning, he decided. Life had become depressingly secure. 'Perhaps not,

Anthony,' he said gently. 'And on the other hand, perhaps there's more to this reported escape than meets the eye.'

'Sir?'

'You can't really see those paranoid Fenians being so careless, can you?'

Keegan was sure no one had followed him. He had entered two stores and changed direction several times in both before making for the older part of the city. He bought three Sunday papers and eight Monday dailies, then walked to a pub beside a small forge-mill. He read too slowly, conscious of the difficulties he had with words. Headlines had their own ambiguities.

Where one newspaper had 'Pile-up at Scotch Corner', another put it 'Articulated Vehicle in Holiday Tragedy'. Nothing was simple. Time dragged on. The columns of newsprint were a sly and shifting barrier. The Sunday morning crash was likely to get into the Monday newspapers. He put them aside as he looked at his watch. Eleven. He had drunk two pints of beer. He had seen two men die. He had almost killed Viney. And he had bought a doll for Ruthie. And he felt quite calm.

His hands were steady enough. The throbbing in his leg had subsided. His tooth felt ragged. The wound in his neck had ceased to hurt. He even felt hungry.

'Two beef sandwiches,' he called to the barmaid. She interrupted her conversation with a couple of office cleaners drinking Guinness to serve him. She was a handsome, full-bodied woman.

'Any mustard, pickles, tomatoes, anything like that?'

Keegan smiled at her. 'Not just now.' She winked at him and Keegan momentarily felt the abrupt and immediate engagement with normal living where a woman's frankly inviting gaze was welcome. He walked back to his newspapers, sensing her disappointment.

He found the reference in a Monday daily. 'Two Injured after Party'. A young couple had crashed at a junction. The time fitted, two-twenty on Saturday morning. It was all there. A temporary traffic island had claimed them. Keegan

98

could see the accident taking place: the young man confident of his skill, aggressive and happy to be cutting up the slower vehicles, his young girl beside him gasping in scared wonder. The warning signs blending into other vehicles' tail-lights, the reflections of neon signs, the dim red lanterns quite lost. A despairing scream from the girl, a last obscenity from the young man and the sudden realization that pain was the only future.

'Are you leaving your papers, love,' said the barmaid.

'I've given up reading.'

'See you again?'

Keegan relented. 'Try to keep me away.'

'I don't think I'd want to.'

Again he checked. No one was following.

A bored inspector handled the inquiry. 'Get this moving, will you, Rawlinson,' he told his sergeant. 'A pick-up for the sly men. Name Keegan, Terence, a Yorkshire address. Check with Records. He's done time a few years back. Apparently he's a bit knocked about. He's a lorry-driver, so particular watch by the patrols.' The inspector looked again at the authorization. 'Make it "Most Urgent". And "Hold without questioning". He'll be heading for London.'

The sergeant set the machinery in motion. Neither man doubted its efficacy. A named and known man travelling to a known destination should soon be found. They would put money on it.

The network of roads sprang to the forefront of his mind. An easy journey. But, again, he was careful. Instinct made him wary. He took a bus to the southern outskirts of the city, then another bus to a big filling station. He waited for the right vehicle.

It came after a twenty-minute wait, an articulated vehicle, its container battered by much handling; Dixon's Container Rentals, Keegan read. The driver was a small sandy-haired Scot, eyes red-rimmed and face crumpled by tiredness. He was glad of company.

'Who're you with?' he wanted to know as the container wagon roared out into the traffic.

'I do relief driving for Merseyliners. Just got back from Belgium. I'm going down to Tilbury.'

'Ye wouldn't fancy an hour at the wheel, would ye? Ah'm done! – had a stopover to see ma mates in Newcastle and noo ah'm pushin' it.'

Keegan flexed his shoulders. The neck wound was closing under the plaster. His shoulder couldn't be cracked after all. The leg had been quiet. 'I'll drive,' he agreed.

And it brought a degree of oblivion. The heavily laden trailer groaned on the steepish Derbyshire hills, but the miles slipped by. Keegan almost forgot the white face and the bandages; for minutes at a time the familiar sights of the road gave him some ease. And it needed concentration, for the weather had changed. Low clouds covered the hills, and rain swirled in a fine spray from the vehicles ahead. The usual unskilled drivers dodged between the trailers, chancing a collision with the thirty-ton monsters as if they were fairground dodgems. Keegan settled to a steady sixty when they came to the motorway, but the easier driving conditions allowed his thoughts to settle. And it was always the white face, the thin bloodless lips and the crushed-butterfly thinness of her body under the sheet. A child – what sort of animal could hurt a child? How could a man, conscious of his strength, bring a child to that pitiful state? The brutal coldness of it brought a thrill of keening fury that was followed immediately by the too-familiar self-condemnation.

He should have known they were the kind to take out insurance for his co-operation. *But how?* Keegan rebelled against the thought. If I'd known they'd be such vindictive bastards I'd have run for it with Ruthie, gone off to one of the coast towns and taken a casual job. Or a harvesting job somewhere. I could have done it, thought Keegan bitterly. Five thousand pounds was too bright a lure. The set-up was so easily seen. Afterwards.

It was the frustrated helplessness that grated. Simply, there was no turning back of the clock. The thing had happened. Ruthie might or might not awake in a few days' time. And, when she awoke, she might or might not have her wits.

Keegan argued with himself: I should have stayed at the

100

hospital. She might have awakened, in spite of what the surgeon said. She could be dying now, surrounded by strangers, the tiny flicker of life dropping away from her: and no one to answer the huge question in her eyes should she return to consciousness for the last time. She was his, he was hers; the long last moment should be for him. Yet who was to say she would awake? Not me, Keegan agonized. I'm no use to her at the hospital.

'Nor here,' he said aloud. The Scot snored back, his mouth slackly open to show his dentures and a tongue thick-coated. Keegan watched a Porsche slide away into the misty spray. 'I'm no use to her there or here. None at all.'

He could not contain the sickness of his fury, so he let his wrists lie on the steering wheel until the pain stung and stung again, driving Ruthie's phantom away, and there was only the numb hatred left. The wheels pounded: *Nider. Graves. Bromley.* And the hours passed.

The police checkpoint was skilfully sited. Traffic had to slow because two lanes were closed for roadworks. A patch of clear road on one of the closed lanes made a convenient layby for the vehicles that interested them. There were four cars and maybe a dozen uniformed policemen, dark coats steaming in the rain. Two policemen were checking a juggernaut's passenger, another was looking into the back of a lorry whose sides advertised office furniture. They were waved on.

Keegan knew at once what had happened. *Viney.* Viney had been unlucky. After all, someone had heard the muffled roar of the two barrels, and the police had been called. The bodies of Brick-boy and the Geordie would now be resting on mortuary slabs. Viney in a cell, rat-mouth clenched as he waited for sly, jolly, gold-toothed Collins, the lawyer who handled all his business, Collins the jovial Welshman who had made such a poor job of Keegan's defence on the assault charge. Keegan looked about him. The rain sheeted down. It might hide him. But where could he go?

On one side, three lanes of traffic took the commuters home, an impassable barrier. And on the other, the police cars waited. He wouldn't make the hard shoulder, never mind the level fields beyond. Not with his torn ligaments.

The traffic police might look overweight but they had their training schedules. No. Not that way.

The Scot awoke. Keegan said:

'They're checking.'

'Oh, God's tiny black boots! If yin load's late ah'm done!'

'If they ask, I'm the driver. There'll be trouble if we switch over now. Where's your papers?'

The Scot weighed the situation up as the stream of traffic filtered through the checkpoint. He didn't like any part of it. There was a new aware look on his sallow face. But all he said was 'Aye. Aye, you gie em these.' And he handed a wallet over.

Keegan saw the scruffy beret at the same time. He took it without asking and crammed his hair tight into it. Then he reached down the side of the cab and wiped grease on to his hand, then on to his face. The bruises merged with the wet film of grease and road dirt. Ahead, the police waved private cars through, as well as local lorries. They knew exactly what they were after.

An irritated constable indicated that a container lorry ahead should pull in. For a moment, Keegan thought he would be waved on. A tight core of vomit fought for release. He choked it down. Also the surging dissatisfaction with his own course of conduct: *a fool's errand!* he shrieked to himself. You let your own daughter be hammered, and now you're caught by the road patrols. They knew they'd get you! You stupid, sodding great fool!

Two of them looked into the cab.

'Passenger here!' one called.

Two more men came forward, faces red from the stinging rain. They were extremely alert.

'Now, sir,' said the tall, heavy sergeant. 'Where might you be heading?'

Keegan saw the folds of flesh, the large nose with hair growing from the tip. It was almost funny. And the sight relieved his sick tension. 'Doon tae Folkestone,' he said, and beside him the Scot stirred in surprise as the lowland Scots intonation rolled out from Keegan's throat.

'Could I see your licence?'

Keegan realized they were more interested in the man

102

beside him. He found his mind racing. He had not thought so fast since his playing days. Without intending it, he had sold the intercepting police a gold-plated dummy. They weren't looking for a driver. The hat, the grease, the fact that he was driving rather than a passenger: it might be enough.

If the Scot kept his head.

On the nearside, a large hand tapped peremptorily. The Scot wound his window down. Keegan heard a deep burr request the Scot to step out. The Scot growled, glared at Keegan, and jumped out into the rain. Keegan watched the sergeant at his side of the vehicle.

'Your full name, sir?' the sergeant said.

'Keith Blair McDougall,' said Keegan. He didn't know the address. The lowland Scots dialect wasn't too convincing, but he did possess some talent for mimicry, unused since schooldays.

'Just checking,' said the sergeant. 'Won't keep you long, Jock.'

He passed the licence back and disappeared from view. Then Keegan heard him talking to the other policemen. The words were drowned in the whine of motorway traffic, and Keegan felt his hands murderously tight on the dash. Moments later, the Scot climbed into the passenger seat, cursing obscenely. He glowered at Keegan.

'Ah'm fuckin' late and ye've nearly got me mah job lost!' he hissed.

'Drive on!' called the sergeant.

Keegan set the vehicle rolling. It had taken perhaps two minutes. Sweat rolled off his face. He itched unbearably over most of his body. The bruises and cuts glowed with pain.

'What the fuck's it aboot?' the Scot demanded.

'You know the fuzz. Always on about some poor sod.'

'But, mon, they said they wanted a pick-up, a lorry-man, and had I seen a big feller up North!'

The Scot knew the score.

Keegan debated: force, bribery, what? The man was physically insignificant; he was a boozer, so he could use money. But neither bribery nor threats would keep him quiet.

'Look, Jock, you're in the clear – right?'

103

'Aye?'

'You've had your rest, the police are satisfied, so why not leave it at that? You say nothing, I say nothing. Both of us keep quiet.' Keegan took off the beret. 'Let it go?'

The Scot's thought processes were easy to follow. Keegan could be wanted for some serious crime, and aiding him meant trouble, concealing the aid worse trouble. If it came out. If not, if Keegan was just a lorry-man going South legitimately, why invite complication by reporting unfounded suspicion to the police? Again, if Keegan *was* a criminal on the run, he would be a desperate man, dangerous even.

In the end, the natural reluctance of the Scots to aid authority decided matters.

'Why, mon, ah'm getting mixed up in nothing! But no word to a fuckin' soul, eh?'

'Right. I want out soon, anyway.'

Yet he did not argue when Keegan drove a mile off the route. Keegan jumped out. Not far now. 'Ah'm not pickin' up ony mair fuckin' hitch-hikers!'

Keegan watched the big artic disappear into the sheeting rain. One tail-light was much brighter than the rest. There was too much black smoke. Dixon's was a badly serviced outfit. Keegan limped towards a shopping complex. The rain had soaked through the sweater and into the plaster on his neck wound. It all seemed to be happening to someone else, someone else's cold and pain. Only the tired bitter vengeance was his own.

Keegan paused at a row of shops. He saw the clothes in the window, then his own haggard, dripping figure. He didn't rationalize his decision. He went in.

The shop was full of bright summer gear for the younger executive. The shop assistants were slim young men, and haughty. It was almost five-thirty.

He bought a stylish brown leather jacket, fawn slacks, a yellow Cashmere sweater, soft brown leather shoes, yellow socks, all expensive.

'And that,' said Keegan. The jaunty trilby would conceal his thick blonde hair. He saw the umbrellas. 'And one of those.' He asked for the changing room and returned in peacock splendour. 'Put these in a bag,' he told the assistant, pulling out the bundle of notes. A quick exchange of glances passed between the two assistants: surprise, envy, curiosity. They would discuss him when he was gone. Not that it mattered. Keegan knew he was within a mile or so of the house. And then that he was taking on camouflage, enough to deflect the interest of the cruising patrols; enough to give him the appearance of the bright young executive. He pitched the sodden bundle into a waste basket outside a grocer's and then went inside to buy a packet of sausage rolls.

He ate quickly, hungrily, careless of the jagged tooth. Rain washed the umbrella. Concealing the limp, he walked swiftly along the leafy road. Memories surged. It was different in a car, but not so much different. He found himself talking as he followed his driver's memories. 'It accelerated *here*,' and *here* was wide and straight, with the cars sweeping by fast; 'then swayed,' and *swayed* for a tight bend, but the commuter traffic barely slowed as brakes were brushed and the shock-absorbers took the strain; 'then fast again,' said Keegan aloud and almost into the face of a bald youth in sandals and a dripping yellow cloak who looked back at him and sang a weird chant. Keegan checked, suddenly brought back to a semblance of reality. He had seen nothing like the youth in his life, ever; but the beaming, shining-wet head was past, the strange chant lingered, reminding him of a day when he had taken Ruthie to the seaside and heard the gulls hoarsely and hungrily calling to the sky and the waves far below. Black fury raged then, blind and bitter. The umbrella seemed a ridiculous thing, the smart clothes a clown's costume: the long journey was near its finish. Dressed so inappropriately, face a mass of bruises, body sore, the cuts opening, Keegan saw himself as a pitiful object. Wishing violence, he wondered if, after all, he could bear it again. He had a sudden, horrific memory of the Geordie crumpling, head ruined, and then Brick-boy slung over Gus's broad shoulder: and then all the images were black violence, red rage, clanging images of steel and blood, and Keegan could hardly walk, so much was his surge of huge, surging hate. In his torment memory misled.

He missed the right turning into the tree-lined lane, and

105

the watchers eased clutch pedals and allowed the cars to slide forward again. Fifty yards after the turning, Keegan stopped. He looked back.

'There,' he said aloud. He angled the umbrella against the driving rain and retraced his steps. The short journey in the car floated through his mind again. After the tight bend, it had accelerated and then turned sharp right. He could almost see the Mercedes rocking hard over and then picking up speed under Bromley's thin, long hands. Keegan exulted. Very near now.

On the road, thick with commuter traffic, two drivers cursed. The cunning of the English bastard! By the time they had cut across the traffic, Keegan was out of sight.

The gates were closed. Black and gold-painted they reared above him, eight feet high, not an insuperable obstacle. There were no passers-by, the lane darkened by foliage threshing in the wind. Keegan put his hand out to take the easy hand-hold. Seconds to get over the gates. He reached and measured the easy step up. His right knee flared with pain. And he saw the green metal box behind the left-hand gate-post. An alarm system. Keegan lowered himself.

Keegan limped on. The walls stretched a hundred yards ahead, topped by bushes and young trees. The alarm system might run along the top of the wall. Keegan trembled with renewed outrage. The bastards were secure, oh they were cautious and cunning! He ran now, for a thick growth of trees overhung the wall, trees bright with summer blossom, but trees with branches thick enough to tread on.

He lowered the umbrella, threw it down, glad to be rid of it, and scrambled for the top of the cold wet brick wall. His neck wound cracked open at once; his shoulder muscles crawled with shooting pains; his ribs brushed the top of the wall and screamed their particular complaint. But he was up, already searching for the wires.

They ran in two lines, one dull-red, the other green; but the thick branches overlay them, so that he had not touched either. Keegan grinned with relief. No signal to the house. Then it came to him that Graves might not be there. Or Nider. Or Bromley. The trek south might be for nothing.

Keegan looked down. The lane was empty except for the

umbrella bellying with wind. He turned and lowered himself from the greasy branches into thick undergrowth, very careful to keep the accelerated weight off his right leg. A thin branch whipped into his face, broad leaves with sharp edges scraped skin away. He stood still, balanced uneasily on a pile of rotten undergrowth. He couldn't see the house. There was no point in waiting and listening. You had to know what you were expecting to hear.

He saw the dog at the same time as the house.

Keegan stopped. It didn't look dangerous. An Alsatian, not big. Black, very unhappy. Just the one. It was sniffing at something in a huge clump of rhododendrons. Its coat glistened with rain. Keegan wished he had a weapon, a pick-axe handle, a heavy chopping knife. He thought he could kill a dog. He looked around, a minimal head movement in a search for a potential weapon. None in sight. No heavy sticks. Just a few rotten twigs. A minute passed. Then the dog turned, its jaws opened. A thin whine of complaint sounded above the roar of the wind and the splashing of water. It must see him. Then it looked back into the rhododendrons. The rain swirled the masses of branches, showering rain on to the dog's glistening fur. There was a human quality about the way it shivered. Keegan's heart pounded. The dog wanted to get out of the rain, like any other warm-blooded creature. Christ, thought Keegan, I might be lucky.

It looked away from him, scanning for movement, a furtive and reluctant watchdog.

Then it crept into the bushes.

Keegan let the air sigh from his lungs. The dog hadn't been able to pick him out against the background of bushes. The brown leather coat had camouflaged him, the rain and wind had dulled the dog's faculties and sent it to shelter. If he kept to the soft darkness of the underbushes, he could keep thirty or so yards from the dog's shelter and then reach the cover of a rose arbour. There had to be a way in.

Keegan moved carefully. The leather of the jacket began to rub his neck. He thought suddenly of Jenny's warmth and the pity in her face. She had offered all the money she had. Another memory followed. Keegan thought: the doll in the cab of the artic. I wonder what happened to it when the

107

police got there. It would be an exhibit probably, a clue. Then he thought of fingerprints all over the cab. It wouldn't take them long to check with the records. No wonder there'd been an alert. If they don't want me for Viney's goons, they'll do me for the artic hijack. Keegan's face twitched. *Graves again.* Graves sending Nider and Bromley to pick up Ruthie. Keegan, not an intellectual, could understand his own feelings at that moment.

He was full of hate. Not many people could hate, not for long. The strain on the nervous system wasn't to be tolerated. Animals couldn't hate. They hadn't the stamina. It took a man like himself, pushed and pushed beyond shock to outrage; a man who had nothing at all to lose. Then it was possible to feel the kind that demanded immediate action. Not the kind of festering grievance Viney and Hagan had nursed for all those years. That was something else again. Keegan knew his own hatred to be relatively clean. Vengeance was a simple condition or feeling. But that's not all, Keegan realized. I have to be sure that they *knew*. That when Nider struggled with Ruthie, he didn't care that she might be injured. That when he and Bromley left her they knew she might die. Keegan felt the tears rising up, grief and rage: if, for one moment, he had thought of the consequences of letting Ruthie out of his sight! He wanted to cry out, but a watcher would not have known it.

His face showed purpose, his movements were sure and steady. He progressed painfully, slowly, but taking no chance of attracting the dog's attention. And, always, he watched the windows of the house for a sign of movement. His senses had never been so alert.

A feeling of elation suddenly touched him. He was at the rose arbour. The dog was fifty yards away, the house only ten paces.

He stepped carefully across the flagged, sweet-smelling arbour. Roses trailed about him, great cabbage-like pinks, most of them cankered. Ahead was the north corner of the house. There would be an internal alarm system, but Keegan had learned something about those in the past. It had been one of his duties to check the club's systems. There was always one door or window with its weakness. More likely the rear. Keegan passed along the north wall and made for the back of the house.

He kept close to the wall and listened before moving around the corner. It was the fierce booming of the wind that made his precautions futile. Bromley almost ran into him. Of all things, he had a waste-bin in his hands. His face was turned away from the lashing wind, or he would have seen Keegan first. As it was, he had the faster reactions.

Keegan's blow was launched, a crude punch to the head. Bromley saw the movement, side-stepped, hurled the bright blue container and its contents at Keegan, and fluidly sprang up with a high-pitched yell. If the kick had landed, Keegan would have been badly incapacitated – crutch stove in, a leg broken, or belly-wall ruptured. But Keegan had played in a rough school. He knew what such a kick meant in his foot-balling days. Months of walking about in plaster, maybe the end of a career. And he too acted in accordance with his training.

As the empty cans, the gaudy wrappings, the greasy ends of food sprayed his face, Keegan kicked for Bromley's groin, meeting the man's spectacular and deadly leap with an old-fashioned defender's answer to dangerous play. Bromley screamed and cannoned off the wall. He suffered enormous, blinding pain, a terrible disappointment, and the knowledge that an amateur had beaten him. He didn't say anything. His hands groped for support, found none, then he slumped, quite slowly, and curled into a tight foetal knot.

Keegan almost fell beside him, for he had used the injured right leg. He leant against the wall, sobbing to catch his breath, hardly daring to think of the damage to the already torn ligament. He knew he couldn't get far. You can't do any more, Keegan, he said to himself, your leg's ruined, you're finished, finished! Beneath him, Bromley found his voice and screamed.

The dog heard and answered. It was the cry of a hunting-beast. Keegan's whole body froze. There was a menace in its throaty answering yell that made him wish to be far away, out of the business, back where he belonged, in the grimy suburbs of an unimportant northern town, back with the things he knew, the lorry, the dishevelled house, the round of pub and easy, well-fleshed women he knew; and Ruthie. *Ruthie.*

The dog yelped, close now. Keegan looked down at the writhing body. Bromley must have a gun. But the dog was close. It would be searching, listening into the roaring of the wind, peering ahead for sign of hasty, guilty movement. It had seemed almost harmless as it made for shelter. But it would know its function. He moved, crab-like, along the wall, willing himself to place the right leg down, to walk fast, and, hearing the dog again, to run. But there was no spring in him, only the awareness of pain. It had all been such a mistake to think he could get to Graves, a mistake to hope for the look in the wizened, sly face that would tell him that Graves regretted what he had done. (For this was what he *had* to see! He knew it then.) Then fear made him move, for the dog was only a few yards away.

Keegan shuffled forward, stumbling against the doorway as the gleaming-coated animal saw him and knew him for an intruder. Bromley's shrill scream held it for a second or two; and so did the food scraps. It looked down, whined, wagged its tail, bared its teeth, a puzzled dog, unsure as to whether to beg for food or chase the intruder. It didn't expect Bromley to be on the floor, nor Bromley, arms flailing, hitting it in the face. Terribly confused, the dog halted, growled; Keegan pushed himself through the doorway and slammed the door behind him. Bromley was yelling again, louder now. There was no one in the room.

It was a kitchen. Large and modern, with gleaming stainless steel fittings. On the stove, a number of pans gave off steam. There was a delicious smell of roasting meat. Keegan held on to a working surface and choked on his laughter. Bromley was, amongst other things, the cook. And now he lay outside, with a sadly puzzled Alsatian whining at him and his balls halfway through his guts. Keegan had been wondering how he would feel if he was ever able to find one of the men who had left Ruthie to die, wondered if he would feel some kind of release: there was none. It had been so quick, so painful, seconds of grotesque fear and violence, and that was all.

A man preparing food had taken a waste-bin into the rain

to make way for more waste. And now he lay writhing. Keegan thought: What if it's the same when I see Nider? Or Graves? What if it makes no difference at all?

But to think like that, to allow that kind of self-questioning, was to give up. If he asked one more question, he must return to the rain, somehow get past the maddened dog, and reach Ruthie before the police picked him up or the Irishmen found him. Keegan shuddered with cold and indecision. He shook his head and rain flew on to the hot-plate and spanged into steam.

There was nothing left to go back to. He said to himself: I'd never make it, not twice. There was no choice to be made when it came to it.

Keegan eased forward on his good leg. Bromley had been using a short-bladed kitchen knife, viciously sharp, needle-pointed. Beside it were the husks of some vegetable he didn't recognize. Keegan took the knife and listened at the kitchen door. If Nider came, he would strike. He slid the door open. The hall stretched beyond as he remembered it, gloomier though, lit only by wall-brackets with thick parchment shades.

There was no hint of movement. Keegan tensed, then set his right foot down. It wouldn't take him far. So, choking with the pain, he made his way into the hall.

There was a considerable choice of rooms to try. On the the right, the porch; to the left probably a dining-room. Ahead, three doorways. Beside the porch a wide stairway with ornately carved bannisters. And still no hint of movement, no sound to betray a presence. The place reeked of affluence, of confidence, of a quiet wealthy superiority. There were oil-paintings of old-fashioned country scenes, harvests and water-meadows; then a series of garish caricatures of long-dead politicians and soldiers. Keegan licked his lips. It was no place for a broken-down truck driver, no matter how good his cause.

But he went on. Stiff with pain and fatigue, he hobbled across the hallway to Graves' study.

There was no way of doing it subtly, nothing but to push the door open and hope to catch them at a disadvantage. He realized that it was not simply a desire for revenge that motivated him, and that he knew more about himself, now in these last desperate hours of his search, than he had ever known before. For one thing he knew that he had taken the knife more as a means of self-protection than an offensive weapon. For another, that he was at the end of his resources.

Luck, some instinct for survival, the storm, the branches overlying the alarm wires – all had brought him so far, but principally luck. It couldn't last. He opened the door.

Adrenalin surged, but to no effect, for the room, though well-lit, was empty. Keegan saw the desk and visualized Graves sitting there: a small aged devil, who transfixed you with his eyes because you knew he thought of you as dead and wondered only at the manner of your taking-off. Bile rose up in Keegan's throat. He thought of Bromley then, and wondered if he was even now painfully struggling to the kitchen door. Or had the dog savaged him? Even as the bitterness of failure brought its attendant despair, Keegan heard the cracked laughter of the man. *Graves!* The sound was one of mockery and self-disgust, a strange querulous hilarity that sent shivers down the back of Keegan's neck.

It came from the doorway to Keegan's left. There was a room beyond the study. He hadn't noticed the doorway before, its green baize blended into the velvet wallpaper. Graves was in there.

Keegan looked down at the knife. It wasn't enough. He should have taken Bromley's gun, for surely he carried one even when he was taking the rubbish away. Keegan looked about. Graves' desk. He crossed, quietly and quickly. The central drawer was locked. There were deeper side drawers.

And they contained only files.

Keegan looked about him. A cabinet behind the desk. He opened it and found rows of drinks. The whisky bottle tempted him, but he didn't reach for it. Graves' weird laughter rang out again, and this time a high-pitched echo followed, a different voice from a deeper chest.

Keegan stiffened. It was Nider. Nider and Graves through the green baize door. Keegan looked into another wall-cabinet. No sign of a weapon. Maps rolled up, some kind of electronic controls (for the security system?), bundles of tape-bound papers, and some more folders. No sign of a

112

weapon – until Keegan saw the plastic tube, and the bulbous conical red and black striped warhead.

He laughed then, for he knew what it was!

The thing looked deadly, light and toy-like as it was. By no stretch of the imagination could it be anything but a rocket-launcher; vicious and deadly. This was what the Irish wanted this was what he had been set up for; this was why Ruthie lay in the Intensive Care Unit.

Keegan's face stiffened.

It was fitting that Graves should see the thing again, but this time pointed at him.

Keegan was a man of his hands. The controls were simple A shoulder-rest, a priming-button, a trigger. It was going to be easy after all.

Keegan crossed to the green baize door, very slow. There was a grim inevitability about it now. He no longer tried to analyse his feeling or his reactions. Graves' terrible laughter had paralyzed his conscious thoughts.

Graves giggled as he pushed the door open. It sounded like a satanic schoolgirl. Keegan held his breath against the sudden blast of hot, damp air. The room was full of steam, in it a wooden bench and on that two grotesque shapes.

Keegan knew of such practices, had heard for himself as in the dark of the cells men sweated in the grotesque parodies of love. He had never imagined it to look like this. It was absurd and sickening, the wizened yet still muscular Graves pinned in the grip of the naked Nider, both men crying out as if in eager pain.

'Christ,' whispered Keegan, forgetting his plan of revenge, forgetting the rocket-launcher in his hands:

'Is this what you are?'

The difficulty was that Nider and Graves didn't seem to be unduly alarmed. Graves was apparently comfortable, round bald head resting on his hands very much in the manner of a sunbather regarding an interesting beach incident. And Nider clambered from the bench, his great folds of muscle and square massive torso almost relaxed.

'What a surprise you've turned out to be, Keegan!' Graves declared. 'Anthony was quite right about you. What have you done with him?'

113

Keegan wondered about the effect of the rocket blast at close range.

'Keep still!' he yelled to Nider. 'Back off to the wall or I'll blow both of you bastards to pieces!'

Nider turned his back and loped to a screen.

'Tell him!' yelled Keegan, the hot air rushing into his lungs and the strange excitement in Graves' eyes dismaying him. It was all going wrong.

'No, Keegan, fire your pop-gun, dear boy!'

Nider was out of sight. He would be back in a second or two with a gun.

'Fire away,' invited Graves.

No time to think now. Keegan backed two paces and gritted his teeth. Nider appeared, still naked, a large automatic in his hand. Keegan pulled the plastic trigger.

He felt the slight recoil. His eyes closed against the blossoming fury. There was a moment's delay. Keegan's senses froze. Then the rocket slid from the plastic launcher, the retaining sprocket released, the slight forward motion brought about by the relaxation of the retaining spring's pressure. The red and black striped rocket slipped free and dropped at Keegan's feet.

Nider was smiling. Graves shook his head.

'Keegan, you're playing in the wrong league,' he said sadly. 'Now, why on earth couldn't you have done what you were supposed to do?'

It was absurdity piled on absurdity. Defeat wasn't just death, it was senseless sacrifice. It was the humiliation of dying at the hands of a giggling old queen and his stud. Nider, who had manhandled Ruthie, would kill him. The end, thought Keegan: I've come so far to die a fool's death.

There was only one thing left.

'Why Ruthie?' he asked, and now he felt all the injuries he had received as a result of Graves' diabolical plan. Ribs, broken teeth, the neck wound, the stabbing pains in his leg; and the sour, unrelenting misery of Ruthie's loss.

'The daughter,' Nider breathed, as Graves looked a question.

'Oh, no one wanted to hurt her,' Graves said. 'It was one of our usual precautions which sadly went wrong. Nider tells

114

me he was a little clumsy for once. Just a part of our normal arrangements, Keegan. We always make sure, don't we, Nider?'

Nider nodded, relaxed but ready. Nider could put half a dozen holes in him before he reached the knife in his pocket. He had his answer to the vast unreason of it all now. No reason at all. Ruthie might die for nothing. There was no malice in Nider, none towards either Ruthie or himself. Ruthie and he were expendable.

'Now tell us what's become of Anthony,' said Graves.

'Outside,' said Keegan, hearing his own voice hollow and unreal. 'In the rain.'

'How bad is he?'

'Bad enough.'

'And you got past the Alsatian too?'

Keegan nodded.

'And our alarm system! Really, we'll have to check them over! We can't have our privacy disturbed like this, can we, Nider?'

Keegan read his own death sentence. He had been dismissed.

'But why Ruthie!' he yelled, driven beyond endurance. 'Why a child!'

Graves smiled at him. 'Why anybody? Nider, I think you'll have to prepare dinner when you've seen to Anthony. I've one or two questions for you, Keegan, when I've dressed. I do hope you've not been indiscreet. Take him away for the moment, Nider.'

Nider motioned just as the alarm bells shrilled through the house; simultaneously a red light began flashing at the far end of the sauna. There was a sound of glass breaking.

Graves leapt to his feet like an agile spider. Keegan threw himself sideways as Nider fired. The bullets spat past him, flat whipcrack explosions and sudden flurries of air. Keegan tried to slam the heavy door on Nider's head. He caught the half-caste's arm and shoulder. Nider screamed and dropped the automatic.

The room whirled as Keegan fell on his right leg. He heard Nider screaming, then his own bellow of agony. He glimpsed figures, several of them, and then the flash of black wet fur.

115

'Hold, hold, Sean, don't shoot the fucker, don't shoot – I want it done right, we're not a bunch of murderers like the Brits!'

It was an Irish voice, educated, but so overwrought that it was coarser than Sean's.

'The dog! The fuckin' dog's got me, sweet Jasus, it's eating me leg off!' yelled a high-pitched voice Keegan had heard before under stress; the youth Kevin.

An explosion rang out, duller, heavier than Nider's automatic. The dog screamed. Keegan tried to get to his feet. He saw a heavy revolver a foot from his face and behind the revolver the ugly cheerful face of the I.R.A. Provo called Sean.

'In there!' screamed another voice, and it was the woman this time, Cynthia, who had copulated with the Mick whilst he lay in hallucinated agony after his beating. 'Through the green door.'

Nider had retrieved his damaged arm.

'More of them!' yelled the educated voice, now more authoritative.

One of the men moved forward, a man Keegan didn't know, middle-aged and very excited. He yanked the back door, keeping out of the line of fire of the other Irishmen. They had experience of this kind of thing. They'd have watched the army patrols. One man was already at the other side of the door, also out of the firing-line. Another crouched, poised to throw himself forward and down, revolver ready. *Liam*, recognized Keegan. Nider hurled himself out, a solid mass of bone and muscle, yellow in the subdued lights, and then already falling as the heavy bullets whumped into his chest and stomach, one, two, three, the last striking bone. Keegan did not hear Nider's death-roar, but he saw the grimace as he died. Smoke snaked from the thin man's automatic.

The explosions shocked and deafened them all.

The silence that followed was appalling.

Gradually, Keegan heard sounds. Sean's breathing as he glared down the foresight of his revolver. Nider's dying reflexes rustling the carpet. Cynthia saying 'Oh, oh, oh!' very softly under her breath. The man with the educated voice, a thin, jerkily moving figure with long, black-grey bushy hair,

116

automatic in hand, moved slowly, a loose board creaking under his feet. Pieces of plaster tapping on the polished floor beyond the edge of the carpet. And a low terrifying sound came from the throat of the dog, not yet dead.

'How many?' whispered the thin man.

Sean jammed the revolver into Keegan's face, bone judder-ing under the impact.

'One,' said Keegan. 'One more.'

'He'll have no gun,' said the thin man quietly, calm now. 'Patrick, take the automatic,' he told the middle-aged man. He gestured to Nider's gun. 'Come out!' he said, raising his voice. 'Come out, you British bastard!'

Keegan could have laughed aloud. After all, Graves was going to die. He was quite sure of it. There was an inevita-bility about it all that he could not have recognized until now. He thought suddenly: I'm going to be killed too. They won't let me live. I'm an informer and an agent, and Graves is my employer. I just wish I'd got the sense, maybe the know-how to have it better. I've got it now, he mused. I could do it right, given my time over again.

There was no answer from the sauna.

Deliberately, the thin man fired twice through the open doorway, aiming high. The noise from the sauna was huge. Dull, booming echoes split the hot air in a series of colossal drumbeats.

'I want to see your face, you that killed a dozen good lads and lost us three-quarters of our arms!' called the I.R.A. leader. 'Come out, or I'll throw a jelly-bomb in!'

Keegan heard a slight cough.

'I'm quite prepared to surrender,' called Graves.

The man beside the doorway tensed. Sean's finger whitened on the trigger. Kevin muttered savagely. Cynthia produced the low, concerned noises she had made before. The thin man moved to the side.

Graves appeared, a large white towel draped about his scrawny frame.

'Honourable surrender, and all that,' he said. 'Geneva Convention and no nonsense about summary execution, what?'

Keegan felt cold again, defeated. Graves was mocking the

117

Provos. He looked like some Indian resistance leader from the days of non-violence, almost a benevolent old gentleman.

'Name?' spat the thin man.

'—rank and number,' completed Graves, unconcerned. 'Ah, Keegan, still with us?'

The thin man looked at his adversary. 'You're the one who had the tracers put in the rockets.' He knew.

Tracers. Keegan thought of the rocket which had failed. A dud. Defused. Of course they wouldn't keep a live weapon like that about. Too dangerous. *Tracers?*

Sean could not restrain his bitterness. Still with the revolver jammed against Keegan's face, he said:

'My own brother was in the Short Stand raid! He died defending the Provisionals' arms against the Brits!'

The thin man breathed hard. 'Get all the files you can. Quick. We'll have half the police in London here in a few minutes. Now,' he said to Graves. 'You and your agent have been condemned by a lawfully appointed tribunal of the Provisional Irish Republican Army for espionage and murder, and I have been appointed to carry out the sentence. There is no appeal.'

He faced Graves. There was a glint in his eye that matched Graves' own strange excitement. Keegan realized that both were acting a part. Both had the same lack of personal involvement in what they faced together. And was all of the Irish tragedy like this? Was it all on the level of murderous farce, with the drums and speeches, the bullets in the head and the back-street raffles for more bullets, the far-reaching organization that brought rockets from Belgium and sent sex-crazed fast-breathing bitches like Cynthia to act as escort?

What were they doing! They liked it, all of them. Sean, ecstatic; Kevin, shaking with murderous lust; Cynthia, her cornflower-blue eyes reckless and; wet the burly heavies, lumpy faces gleaming. All infected with the cancer of violence. All actors in the macabre spectacle of the coming murder, all wondering about the limits of their own ruthlessness.

Graves smiled past the thin man. 'Now, Anthony,' he said.

The room filled with staccato explosions.

Unbelievably, the thin man's eyes bulged and he reached forward as if to embrace Graves. His pistol jammed against Graves' skinny belly. Keegan saw that much, just as Sean did. The dead man's finger jerked, and Graves was hurled back by the heavy bullet. There was a wound like a poppy in his stomach.

Sean gobbled. Noises came from him, but he was too shocked to act. Keegan knocked the revolver away. It fell on to the carpet. Sean realized what was happening but he was too late, for Keegan knew he had a chance of survival. *Anthony.* The tall agent should have been lying in the rain trying to nurse feeling into his shattered crutch.

Someone was screaming as Keegan lashed out at Sean. *Cynthia*, he registered. More shots, more abrupt red flashes, more jangling echoes. Keegan saw Sean stagger to his feet and then slam back against the wall. He avoided the collapsing body. Desperate but no longer despairing, Keegan crawled away from the gunfire, towards the revolver Sean had jammed into his mouth.

'Aah, Jasus, I'm shot dead!' screamed one of the Irishmen: Kevin, a true prophet, blood spouting from his throat.

'Michael! Sean!' came Cynthia's answering yell.

Keegan grabbed the revolver and faced the smoke-filled room. Nose, throat, ears were full of the screaming and echoing thunder. He saw Bromley wave an odd-looking automatic, something between a pistol and a machine-gun, and then smile sweetly before he fell on his face.

The upper-class whore was on her hands and knees beating the carpet beside the body of the thin Provo leader. She wasn't screaming any more. Keegan saw Sean get to his feet, right arm clutching his side. Another of them was regaining his senses, this one unwounded. It was the docker called Liam. Another Irishman lay riddled in a growing dark pool beside the body of the Alsatian. Sean and the docker glared around them. It had taken maybe thirty seconds.

'Him!' yelled Sean, waving his arm at Keegan. 'Shoot the informing bastard! He's lawfully dead, he has to be killed!'

The docker's pistol was at his feet, dropped in the noise as he dived away from Bromley's odd automatic. He looked down, and then at the revolver in Keegan's fist.

119

'He's killed the Commandant,' whimpered Liam. 'Sean, his back's shot right away, his backbone's broken with the bullets, God help us!'

Sean tried to rally him. 'Can't you see that one's nothing – go for his gun or we're dead men too!'

Keegan felt the revolver shaking in his hand. Corpses littered the room. The dog tried to die. Cynthia was trying to pray to him, hands together like a little girl, her wild blue eyes ringed white as she stared up at the revolver's black mouth.

They expected to be shot dead, all of them. All that were left alive. Keegan glanced about him. Graves wasn't dead, not yet. There was something in the expression of his face that proved it, yet he wasn't going to open his eyes. One wizened hand opened and closed like a crab's claw.

But Nider was dead, stone-dead. And Bromley could not last long. Keegan saw the blood of the Alsatian run to join another spreading pool.

He said:

'Listen, you crazy bastards, I never was part of this set-up, I never wanted to be part of it, I'm just an ordinary truck-driver – nothing to you!'

'You led the pigs to our stores all over Belfast!' yelled Sean. 'Youse set the Army on to us, ya dirty informer, and youse is dead, stark dead though youse still breathe! Youse knew the tracers in the rockets would find our lads, and me own brother's lying stone-cold on account of it! Ah, we know you, and we'll get you!'

Keegan quailed before the venomous attack. He held the revolver forward more as a shield than a threat.

'Be quiet, Sean, he'll shoot!' screamed Cynthia.

Keegan heard. The voice got to him through the panic which made him want to pitch the revolver to Sean and ask him to end it.

'Someone's got to believe me,' he said, his mouth quivering. 'I was set up, nothing more! I just wanted to ask them why Ruthie – why they hurt my daughter!'

Cynthia slowly got to her feet.

'He means it, Sean, maybe we've made a mistake!'

120

'That's it,' said Liam. 'Aisy on him, Sean. Isn't that enough of killing?'

Keegan missed the imploring look on Cynthia's face, and the rapid understanding between her and the thickset Irishman.

Sean groaned and held his side. 'You wouldn't be codding us? We've three dead, maybe four. You wouldn't be giving me any double talk?'

'I just want out of it!' Keegan shouted. 'I'm no bloody agent! Keep your war! I'm no part of it, nor want any of it! Do your killing in Ireland, run your guns where you like, but don't come near me again!' He thought of Ruthie. 'Haven't I lost enough through you? *I'm no bloody murderer!* All I want is to be left alone!'

Sean nodded.

'All right, then.' He turned to the docker. 'Aah, for God's sake, let's get the living to a doctor and the Commandant back to Ireland, God help him! We'll have the polis about us in minutes. Away now!'

Keegan again looked down at the revolver. He was very conscious of the docker's stare. 'So it's finished?' he asked Sean.

And how could it be? Yet he hoped, magically, it would all come right.

'We've carried out our orders,' said Sean. 'There's no more to be done.'

Keegan shook his head. He looked about the room again. Graves' eyes were open now, but his hand was not moving. The dog twitched, its blood still pumped into the pool. The middle-aged Irishman called Patrick was groaning. Keegan realized that Sean was waiting for him to decide not to shoot the rest of them.

Keegan limped across the room.

'Then I'll go,' he said. 'I never wanted any part of it!'

He backed away from them. Sean and the woman watched. The docker bent to help his mate. Keegan's mind whirled. He still had difficulty in believing that it was over. The hours had drained him of the ability to feel relief, his injuries refused to allow him to accept that his part was done: his mind blazed, his body shrieked, his nerves felt, each of

121

them, alive with a separate white-hot needle at the end.

Limping, sidling, the revolver too heavy now, he reached the porch. He thought: I didn't want this either. Aloud he said: 'Why did it happen? And I still don't know *how* they could have left her, not a child, not a *child*!'

The door was stiff, but he managed it. There was no sign nor sound of pursuit, no danger from Sean or Liam, certainly not from Cynthia. Keegan felt the rain slash at his neck as he opened the door wide.

He thought he dropped the revolver because it was heavy, but that wasn't so. In fact, a police truncheon neatly paralysed his arm and that was enough to make him reel into the arms of two plain-clothes officers.

'That's one,' he heard someone say.

'You've got it wrong,' he began, and then he realized the futility of it all and waited for the long, slow night to begin. There was never any good to come from arguing with officialdom.

THURSDAY

After almost a complete day Keegan accepted the fact of his survival, then of his arrest.

It was a remand cell, comfortable enough. The meals came regularly, his wounds had been inspected and dressed. There was piped music, a flush lavatory, soap, towels, half a dozen paperback novels and a pack of cards. The doctor who inspected his wounds was brusque and efficient. He even noticed Keegan's broken tooth and said it had to be capped or he'd lose it. He decided that the ribs and shoulder were whole, but that the finger was broken. The leg needed treatment.

No one would answer questions, though.

After eighteen hours, Keegan said to the round-faced officer who brought him his evening meal:

'If I don't hear about Ruthie in the next hour, I do my best to get out.'

The broad red face showed no change of expression.

Keegan said:

'She's in hospital. Those that put her there are dead, both

122

of them.' Quietly he added, 'I want you to tell the others what I said. Ruth Keegan, in one hour.'

It worked.

Keegan knew he was in London, somewhere underground, one of the big remand jails in the centre. There had been no charge, no questions. Keegan could take no more of isolation, of waiting, of not knowing. He was aware of his own state of mind, aware too that there was no possible way in which he could help Ruthie.

Viney had been right, as usual.

He was due for a thirty year stretch. Half of Ruthie's life would be over when he got out; if she had half a lifetime to live. If she knew what that life was. Vengeance had sustained him for the necessary number of hours. That was accomplished, done, finished. No more rage.

Not if they would just tell him.

'This way, Keegan,' said the round-faced man.

Keegan followed. He was surprised to find that there were only four cells on the corridor. And it hadn't the look of a gaol. Nor the stink. The doors, steel inside, were faced on the outside with varnished wood. The corridor was carpeted in some kind of artificial fabric. There was no music in the corridor. At the end of it an ordinary, but heavy oak door opened as they approached.

'Go on, Keegan,' said the round-faced officer. He pushed. Keegan found himself in a large, well-lit modern office.

'Thank you, Cavendish,' said the man at the metal desk.

Keegan stared. It wasn't a nick. He thought: I'm not on remand. They should have charged me. I'm not in gaol, not in a sodding nick! Against his will, he found his spirits rising. He took in what he saw. At the desk, a large, florid-faced man, maybe fifty or so, maybe more. Filing cabinets, papers everywhere, two typewriters on smaller desks, three telephones, one red, the others grey. On the wall, a calendar: a Japanese girl emerging from the sea, every curve and muscle sweetly outlined. Puzzlement chased across Keegan's mind, then a realization.

'Well, Keegan, got to it yet?' asked the man.

Another Oxford poof. Plummy-voiced, supercilious, calm,

contained. Oh God help me, thought Keegan: I'm safer in gaol. He heard himself saying:

'I don't want to hear it, not any of it! All I want to know is how's Ruth.' He took a step forward and saw no increase in tension in the man's demeanour. 'My daughter!' he yelled, suddenly unable to control himself. 'Ruth Keegan.'

The man held up his hand.

'That's enough for now. Listen without talking.' He didn't wait for Keegan to agree. 'I've been on the phone to the hospital within the last ten minutes. Your daughter is going to recover—'

'Thank Christ—'

'—but there are no guarantees about her future condition.' And now the man waited. 'She'll be out of the Intensive Care Unit in another couple of days. After that, it's wait and hope.'

'I want to see her.'

And now there was a pause. 'You know what this is about, don't you, Keegan?'

Keegan was clearer of mind. A bargain. He examined the man more closely. Shirt not too clean. Suit heavy tweed. Thick grey hair well-greased but dirty. Eyes bloodshot. Maybe a drinker. A paunch below the desk: one good punch and he'd fold. Keegan glanced sideways and saw that the further door was ajar.

'Don't be silly, Keegan,' the man said. 'Names first. I'm Mr Holmyard. Want to sit down?'

'Thanks.'

'Now. First, do you believe me about your daughter?'

'I want to see her.'

'I didn't expect you to trust me.' The man called Holmyard tapped the desk. Dirty fingernails. 'You shouldn't trust anyone, not after what you've been through. Here.'

He opened a drawer and threw something on the desk.

Keegan was on his feet, fist balled, tensed to throw himself forward as the obscene thing bounced into his lap. It was the doll, the brutally savaged doll which Ruthie called Miss May.

'Sit down!' he heard. 'Sit down!'

Keegan's rage subsided. Dimly, he heard footsteps retreating behind him. Holmyard wasn't taking chances.

'I had it brought from the lorry,' the man was saying. Keegan's tears rolled on to the doll. 'I know what you're suffering. I can and I will arrange for you to see your daughter. Understand, Keegan?'

A stinking bargain. Keegan wept for himself too. It wasn't the end at all. He choked back the bile and pushed a hand across his face.

'Right,' he said. 'What do you want?'

'It's more what you want, Keegan.'

Both men waited.

'Well?' said Keegan. He knew he would do what he was asked.

'You face any number of charges,' said Holmyard. 'You know as well as I do. You've left a lot of loose ends to tidy up, a surprising number. There's something I want you to understand before we talk. This before anything else. You see, Keegan, you're dead.'

Keegan actually grinned.

'What's funny?' asked Holmyard equably.

'You're the third person who's said that to me in the past couple of days.'

'If one was an Irishman, believe me, he meant it.'

Keegan thought of Sean. 'But they said it was finished!'

'For them it is. The three Irishmen apprehended by the police will spend a long time in gaol, if they're not amnestied when we settle the Irish problem, next year or next century. The Honourable Cynthia Haydon might get away with a year or so. She's a misguided but nevertheless well-connected member of the English aristocracy. But you, Keegan, you're marked. When they were questioned, Sean Cassidy was very insistent that you be told you wouldn't get away with spying or informing.'

Even in his present predicament, Keegan felt the chill of the grave. 'I let them go.'

'No use. You can't ever convince an Irishman once he's got an idea in his head. Not about this sort of thing. Why, they're still killing off informers from the nineteen-twenties. God knows when the reprisals for today's troubles will end. Keegan, they'll get you if you stay in this country. It's a matter of honour with them.'

125

Keegan thought: Those sadistic Micks and *honour*?

'Gaol or work for me,' said Holmyard.

'Graves said that, more or less.'

'And he's dead. He set you up – quite a usual arrangement, I assure you, Keegan, not that we'd do anything like that, of course. You see, Graves needed to prove that he was serious about the load of rocket-launchers. He served you up on a plate to distract the Provos' attention from the possibility of tracers. So they wouldn't even think of the launchers as suspect. Oh, the Army were *very* happy with the results of the operation. *You* should have ended up in a ditch with a couple of bullets in your head and a bit of notepaper in your teeth. Graves misjudged things a little. The Provos followed you, and you found the Section house.' Holmyard opened another drawer. 'Drink? You deserve one.'

'They followed? I was careful—'

'They're experts, Keegan. They put their best men on it. And, as a matter of fact they've put their top hit-man on your trail. A compliment really. Here.'

Keegan sipped the whisky, not enjoying it.

'Want to start talking? Tell me about the loose ends? I can start sweeping up the pieces quickly. We're a rather more comprehensive organization than Graves' Section. More specialized. Well?'

Keegan told it all. Viney's years-long insidious persecution; Graves' offer; the Provos; the final encounters. He left out nothing.

'Knew a good deal of it, of course,' said Holmyard as he refilled Keegan's glass. 'Graves was trespassing on my patch. It's a nasty business you're coming into.' He didn't dislike telling Keegan that. 'There's no room though for little outfits like Graves' Section. We're entirely viable though.' He drank deeply. 'Off his rocker, Graves,' Holmyard went on. 'Got a persecution complex. He thought his Section was due to be closed down.' He drank with relish. 'It was. We found some photographs of a Treasury official who was doing a bit of investigation into his finances. Tortured, I'd say to see what he'd found out. Nasty pictures. Very paranoiac, Graves. He did so want to stay in business.'

Keegan recognized the look on Holmyard's face. There

was Viney's almost gleeful lust to know the weakness of others; but more than that. Holmyard had power too.

'What use will I be?'

'Direct, eh, Keegan?' Holmyard frowned. 'I'm not sure. You're untrained, but that can be remedied. All I can say is that you've got perseverance and luck. There's a little job that's about right for you. Just right. You see, you're a new face. That's important. Faces get known too quickly.'

Keegan could have been excited at any other time. Now, he felt sad, lonely, bitterly frustrated: knowing that he was again a thing to be used. Viney: Graves: now Holmyard. Each had a grip. Each grip got tighter. Now Holmyard was going to set him up. How else could it be? A crock-legged footballer, gaoled bouncer, failed contractor, a man who bungled a murder attempt – Keegan looked into his glass and said to himself: The bastards aren't going to beat me, none of them, try as often as they like. It would be Keegan-patsy all over again, but he had got away with it before and anyway what was the alternative? And there was no way out: none.

He surprised Holmyard. He looked almost happy.

'At least I can see Ruthie.'

Holmyard considered. 'There's that to it.'